FORBIDDEN
TERRITORY

Forbidden Territory

Dr. Hardy ME Mysteries Episode 4

WILLOUGHBY HUNDLEY III

Forbidden Territory
Dr. Hardy ME Mysteries Episode 4

iUniverse books may be ordered through booksellers or by contacting:

iUniverse
1663 Liberty Drive
Bloomington, IN 47403
www.iuniverse.com
844-349-9409

ISBN: 978-1-6632-6999-7 (sc)
ISBN: 978-1-6632-7000-9 (e)

Print information available on the last page.

iUniverse rev. date: 01/28/2025

Thanks to my father, Billy Hundley, and our alma mater,
Hampden Sydney College

CHAPTER 1

"**D**amn! Stupid computer!" exclaimed Dr. Hardy. He stood, frustrated, at a computer station in the South Hill Emergency Room. The mouse arrow had drifted off the tiny one-mm-sized lettering, dwarfed by the 21-inch flat screen monitor. This opened an erroneous charting pathway costing him three penalty clicks to recover.

Dr. Obie Hardy was a seasoned, middle-aged physician who had trained in a pre-computerized era. The Cerner system was the fourth electronic record system that had been thrust upon him in this ER. He had done work in other ERs and clinics that had introduced him to three additional systems. Each version was akin to acquiring another language.

"Why are the characters so *small*?"

"Chill, Doc," said the ER technician. She handed him a sheet of pink-checkered paper. "Here's the EKG for the chest pain patient in room 7." The ER techs did much of the hands-on work in the ER. They started IVs, drew blood for labs, and attached patient monitors.

"Thanks," said Hardy, half-heartedly.

He made a brief assessment of the man in room seven and returned to his electronic oppressor. As he clicked on the icons in the chest pain protocol, he was encumbered by needing to list the reasons for ordered items. He glanced up at the clock, overlooking the miniature digital "6:05 PM" in the lower corner of his screen.

He now had less than an hour to form diagnoses and dispositions for his four patients. It was doubtful he would be done when his shift was scheduled to end at seven.

"Dr. Hardy," said the unit secretary. "There's a call for you from 9-1-1 on 25."

"Okay. Thanks." He guessed that it was a scene where EMS was requesting permission to cease resuscitation on a dead person. "Dr. Hardy here," he answered.

"Are you available for a scene visit?" the caller asked. "We need an ME."

"Well, I won't be free for at least an hour."

"Okay. I'll notify the officers."

"Where is the scene?"

"It's in Chase City. On Main Street."

Dr. Hardy wrote down the address before saying, "I'll call you when I'm en route."

He hadn't brought his medical examiner (ME) bag to work with him, so he had gathered some syringes and blood-sample tubes from the hospital stock. It was 7:25 before he was able to leave the hospital. Since it was May, daylight saving time was in place. One benefit of working the day-shift rotations in the spring and summer was having some sunlight left when getting home from work. *I guess it'll be dark when I get home tonight*, he thought.

The road from South Hill to Chase City ran through farms and fields that were common in rural southside Virginia. There were nine churches scattered along the twenty-mile route. Hardy had nicknamed this stretch the "Church Road." Entering Chase City, he found two county police cruisers parked on Main Street in front of a vacant store building.

As Hardy got out of his Jeep, he was met by two officers. The tallest one stood over six feet and was well known to Hardy as Detective Bruce Duffer. He was the first to speak.

"Hudson," he said, addressing the other officer. "This is one of our county MEs, Dr. Hardy."

"Hudson?" said Hardy, extending his hand.

"That's right, Dr. Hardy," he said as they shook hands. "Detective Duffer here is showing me the ropes." Hudson was a black man appearing to be in his late twenties, medium height.

"Well, he's a good one to follow. He probably has over twenty years of experience. So, what have we got here?" said Dr. Hardy.

Duffer began his report as they walked to the store entrance. "This is a 54-year-old man whose last address is in New York state. Witnesses say he's been living in this vacant store for two or three weeks. He was last seen outside the building yesterday morning. The clerk at the service station next door called it in. He would usually come by their store every day."

They walked inside into subdued lighting. Dr. Hardy flipped up the light switch on the wall.

"No electricity," said Duffer, explaining the persistent dimness.

"Of course," said Dr. Hardy. *Why would there be?* he thought. He noted a human figure on the floor to their right.

"That's him," said Duffer.

Hardy rushed in to begin his exam, hoping to best utilize the failing evening light. The body was lying on its left side, almost face down. He appeared to be a middle-aged, light-skinned black male. He was dressed in a dirty white T-shirt, dark pants, and sandals. Dr. Hardy placed a thermometer in the right armpit. He noted the stiffness of rigor mortis throughout the body, indicating that the time of death was at least six hours earlier. It would be three to four days before the rigor would leave the corpse.

"Have you taken photos?" asked Hardy, even though he was certain that Duffer had.

"Yeah, Doc. About twenty shots," answered Duffer.

"Okay. Let's roll him onto his back."

The decedent, Hardy estimated, was about five nine, 180 pounds. When they turned him, he noted there was some distortion of the facial features from the body positioning. Some brown liquid oozed out of his mouth. A line of ants was crawling up his shirt to his mouth and nose. Duffer flashed a few additional facial photos. Hardy palpated the bones and lifted up the shirt, assessing for evidence of trauma.

"No obvious injuries," announced Dr. Hardy, as he removed the armpit thermometer. "78 degrees. He probably died between 2 and 6 AM."

"We found these prescription bottles," said Officer Hudson. He handed the bottles to the doctor. "They are empty, filled in New York."

Dr. Hardy read the bottles – Stelazine, an anti-psychotic and Depakote, a mood stabilizer. "It looks like he had schizophrenia or bipolar disorder," he thought out loud. "Let me contact the central office and see what they think. Out-of-state doctor, unwitnessed death, probably needs an autopsy."

While awaiting a call back, Dr. Hardy walked about the vacant store. There were no signs of garbage or toilet waste.

"There's no water service either," said Detective Duffer. "I guess he used the bathroom in local stores."

The investigator from the Office of the Chief Medical Examiner (OCME) called Dr. Hardy back. They agreed that an autopsy was needed. Reading from the ID card Officer Hudson had given him, Dr. Hardy said, "The decedent's name is Jon Griffin." He was somewhat relieved that he didn't need to draw fluid samples, as it was now almost dark. "Okay, I'll fax you the scene diagram."

"So, he's going to Richmond. Right, Doc?" asked Duffer.

"Yes. And I'm headed home."

Mecklenburg County was nearly one hundred miles from Richmond. OCME investigators were too far away to make scene visits there feasible. These duties were delegated to area physicians who agreed to perform these services. Even though this was largely a public service, the local MEs were paid a stipend for each case.

While Dr. Hardy drove home, he wondered why this man had been staying locally. Did he have relatives or family connections to this area? When he arrived at his house outside of Boydton, it was fully dark. He used the interior dash light to read the odometer, recording his ME mileage. He logged over 300 miles annually on ME duties. Hardy gathered his notes to carry inside and complete the death report. As he came inside, he was greeted by his wife, Lucy.

"So, you're home," she said.

"Yeah. Had an ME case in Chase City."

"Oh." She glanced toward the kitchen. "I went ahead and ate without you. I fixed you a plate."

So, it's dark when I get home, and I missed eating with my wife, he thought. "Okay," he said, gratefully.

CHAPTER 2

After a seven-day work week, Monday was Dr. Hardy's first day off. He took this opportunity to get his hair cut. For this purpose, he drove over to the Clarksville Barber Shop. It was a one-room shop with two pedestal barber seats on one side and chairs lining the opposite wall. Patrons would sit there awaiting their turns. Two men were seated ahead of him when he entered. *Not bad for a Monday*, he thought.

The lone barber, Derek, smiled and nodded to Hardy as he found himself a seat. He perused the collection of magazines on the table by the front window – guns, fishing, country living. He settled on the local weekly newspaper, *The News Progress*.

The front page headline read: "Solar Energy Proposal Presented to Board." The article reported that the board of supervisors had reviewed a plan to build a solar panel field. The intended site was along the banks of the river below the dam. Dr. Hardy remembered a similar proposal three years earlier targeting the northern portion of the county. It failed due to public fears of ruining the agricultural plains and woodlands, both aesthetically and recreationally. Mecklenburg County contained a large portion of the fifty-thousand-acre lake reservoir and over ten thousand acres of public parks and wildlife management areas. A three hundred-acre solar field would hardly have ravaged the forests.

The barber made short order of the two heads waiting. The

second customer in the barber chair spoke. "I see you've got two chairs here. Are you planning to bring in a partner?"

"Well, no, Pete. But I did have an offer," said Derek. "This girl with orange and purple highlights in her hair, nose and eyebrow piercings, and tattoos came in one day. She said she could double my business. I told her I had all I could do already. She said she was a *cosmetologist*. I offered to let her rent the second chair. She hasn't been back. I think she wanted *me* to pay *her*!"

"You think she'd do my nails?" said Pete, laughing. "My toenails look like cakes of sawdust!"

Derek turned the chair to face the mirror. "How's that, Pete?"

"Well, there's only one thing wrong with this haircut."

"What's that?"

"You left all that gray in there!"

As Pete stood up and handed him some cash, Derek said, "Thanks. All right, Doc. You're next."

As Dr. Hardy climbed onto the chair, he thought of Mr. Bass, the predecessor town barber. He had been a crusty old man who always had a twinkle in his eye. He was an old-school-type barber.

"I remember old man Bass," said Hardy. "He told me once before, while hot shaving my neck, 'Doc, I've probably taken off more moles than you.' He just grinned and held up his straight razor."

"Yeah. And he was probably right!" said Derek.

"Hey. Whatever happened to that skull he kept on the shelf in the shop?"

"Oh, that? He claimed it was an old Indian skull. He found it while he was hunting for arrowheads. I think his wife donated it to Occoneechee State Park."

"Really?"

"Yeah. I think it's on display in that museum gift shop they got there."

"I'd like to see that sometime."

"Well, they've got that powwow out there this month, you know."

"Yeah. That's right." It had been ten years since Hardy had attended the annual powwow. "Maybe I can go then."

By that Saturday, Dr. Hardy had convinced his wife to attend the event with him. The powwow was scheduled from 10:00 AM to 4:00 PM. They parked in the lot by the amphitheater. It was a warm spring day with only a light breeze and very few clouds. The activities were centered in a grassy field, still colored with the vivid green of the season's fresh growth. There were tables and booths set up surrounding a large teepee. The vendors were selling native American items, such as feathered headdresses, blankets, dream catchers, and art work. There was a war paint area for kids to have their faces painted. One spot with a tent-like shade canopy sold musical items, such as handmade flutes, drums, and CDs of Indian recordings. Children made up much of the crowd, running excitedly about. The powwow had a festive feel.

A man in a feathered headdress stood in front of the teepee. He was of medium build having straight, black hair with gray highlights visible above his ears, just beneath his head wear. His thick eyebrows accented his deep tan skin. Western-style embroidery brightened his white dress shirt in contrast to his plain blue jeans.

Holding a microphone, he spoke to the visitors. "Welcome everyone to the fifteenth annual Occoneechee Powwow," he said. "I am Tom Heathcock, chief of the Weyanoke tribe. The Weyanoke, also called the Enos, originally lived near here, on an island in the river you call Roanoke. It is now the head water of Buggs Island lake. But our ancestors were driven from this area over three hundred years ago.

"We now live on the twenty-five-acre Weyanoke reservation in eastern North Carolina. Each year we return here, to the land of our fathers, to celebrate our heritage. The powwow is a homecoming for us." The crowd had grown quiet listening to Chief Heathcock's story. "So now, in celebration, we will dance."

A man was seated beside him, wearing a leather vest and jeans. He had a drum between his knees and began pounding out a rhythm. *Pum-pum-pump, pum-pum-pump.*

"Come. Dance with us!" said the chief, setting his microphone down. He began to walk in stomping steps, to the beat of the drum. *Pum-pum-pump, pum-pum-pump.* Children were the first to join the dance, but soon a ring had formed, encircling the teepee.

Dr. Hardy took Lucy by the hand and said, "Come on, squaw. Let's dance!"

She was reluctant at first, but said, "All right," as he dragged her out into the circle.

"Show me your Native heritage," he commanded.

"Well, you know I'm one-eighth Indian," she said, giving the Seminole tomahawk chop with her hand.

"I know!" agreed Hardy. "I've seen you on the warpath!"

They stomped along to the pounding of the tom-tom until they completed a lap. Dr. Hardy remembered why he had wanted to come to the powwow. "Oh! Let's go up to the museum," he said, as they exited the dance ring. "I haven't seen it yet."

"Okay," she said.

They walked the quarter mile to the museum since Hardy suspected there would be no parking nearby. His suspicions were correct as the parking area was overflowing. In the museum entrance was a gift shop. They walked through the store to reach the exhibit area in the rear. There stood a full-scale human figurine in period Indian dress. Artifacts were on display in glass cases, and recorded historical narrations could be played by pressing button activators.

The Wyanoake were trappers and traders whose furs were a valued commodity. They also provided guide and porter services for travelers and explorers. They were attacked in 1676 by

Nathaniel Bacon's followers as part of Bacon's Rebellion. Scattered and downtrodden, they joined up with other tribes in Virginia and North Carolina. By 1715, their population had dwindled to less than one hundred, and they gathered in a fort in Brunswick County. Fort Christianna had been established for the local Indians by the governor of Virginia.

"Lucy, look at these arrowheads," said Dr. Hardy. He was admiring the triangular stone relics on display.

"Projectile points," she said.

"What?"

"Projectile points. Some are spearheads and tomahawks too."

"Oh, yeah. I see."

In a glass-enclosed case, he found what he was searching for. A brown-colored skull with six partial teeth and no jaw bone. There was a prominent crack along the left side, in the parietal bone.

"That's the skull!" he exclaimed.

"The skull?" she asked.

"Yes! It sat on a shelf in the barber shop for years. Old man Bass always said it was an old Indian skull. Look here." He pointed at a small plaque on the case.

It read: "Artifacts donated by the estate of Mr. Bass."

CHAPTER 3

Dr. Hardy looked up at the wall clock in the South Hill ER. It helped break the eye strain from staring at his computer screen. The round clock with hour and minute hands seemed to make time a tangible entity, not a group of four digits on a display. It was 1:15 PM. He hardly needed to check, however, since the ER was packed and he was hungry. The usual meal-time influx of patients was as predictable as if the ER was a restaurant.

Maybe I could grab my protein drink, he thought. As he returned from the break room with his 30-gram liquid lunch, he heard the EMS radio.

"Chase City 41 to South Hill ER, how do you copy?"

One of the nurses answered the call. "South Hill ER. Go ahead Chase City."

"We have a thirty-two-year-old male who was injured in a car explosion. He has second-degree burns on his face, chest, and arms." The report continued with vital signs and treatments including IV fluids and pain medication. "ETA 8 minutes. Any further, South Hill?"

"No further, Chase City. Trauma 2 on arrival."

"A car explosion?" said Dr. Hardy.

"Yes! That's what they said," answered the nurse.

"I've never seen one of those here before." He hastily began completing the chart on his vomiting patient, preparing for their discharge. He needed to be ready for this incoming emergency.

As he took a gulp of his vanilla nectar, he mentally reviewed the Parkland formula for fluid resuscitation of burn victims. *1-2-3-4,* he thought. *½ the fluid over the first 3ʳᵈ of the day, totaling 4 ml/kg times the percentage BSA (body surface area) burned.* As he printed the discharge papers, he heard the beeping sound of an ambulance backing up to the ER.

The ambulance bay doors slid open and the EMTs pushed their stretcher through and into the Trauma 2 treatment area. Their passenger moaned as he was rolled up beside the ER cot.

"He was lucky," said one of the EMTs. "It appears he got mostly flash burns and not blast injuries."

"But about 20 percent body surface burns," added the second attendant.

"He's had 100 mics of fentanyl."

They slid him onto the ED cot, and Dr. Hardy began assessing his injuries. He was a hefty white male with a goatee. His face was reddened, and his eyebrows and beard were singed, casting an odor of burnt hair. He was able to answer questions, and there was no soot in his eyes or throat. *No signs of inhalation injuries,* thought Hardy. There were blisters on his hands and forearms. His shirt had apparently protected his torso somewhat, as the skin was only reddened, much like a sunburn.

"You need to be treated at a burn center," Dr. Hardy said to the man. "We will make the arrangements to send you there."

As Dr. Hardy left the exam room, he found Detective Bruce Duffer standing in the hallway. He wore a white golf shirt with a sheriff's star monogram.

"Is it okay to talk with him now?" he asked.

"Yeah. He can talk," said Dr. Hardy. "So, how did this car explode?"

"Well, the explosion was confined to the trunk."

"Oh." Hardy thought of maybe road flares, a spare fuel jug, or an auto battery.

"A mobile meth lab!"

"No! Really?"

"Yep. They use propane to heat hydrochloric acid and bubble the vapor into the base liquid. It makes the meth precipitate and form crystals."

"No shit? In a car trunk?" said Dr. Hardy. It was unbelievable that someone would put such a volatile concoction in their trunk.

"Well, it's certainly not an ideal place." Duffer nodded to Trauma 2. "Case in point."

Dr. Hardy returned to his computer to enter the orders for IV fluids, pain medication, and a tetanus vaccination. He took another swallow from his protein beverage. *Great! It's gotten warm now!* As he was completing the transfer form, Duffer walked over to him.

"I've arrested him," he said to Dr. Hardy.

"Is he in cuffs? His forearms are burned."

"Yeah. I cuffed his ankles. How will he be traveling?"

"He's stable enough for ground ambulance," said Dr. Hardy. He suddenly remembered their last case together. It had seemed a bit bizarre. "Oh, by the way, any word on the man from the vacant store last month?"

"Well, I did learn some things. Seems the store is owned by his aunt and three other relatives. Part of an inheritance. He was here for the powwow. It seems he was a Native American and lived on an Iroquois reservation in New York state."

"Interesting. So, what did he die from?" asked Dr. Hardy.

"Since he was fifty-three years old and there was no evidence of foul play found, they called it *natural causes.*"

CHAPTER 4

Dr. Hardy began his week off with a cup of coffee on his back porch. He felt a bit lazy after working a seven-day stretch. As he sipped his coffee, he looked over the weekly county newspaper, *The News Progress*, from the past week.

The front page headline read: "Supervisors Consider Solar Power Zoning." Radiant Acquired Energy (RAE) had petitioned to rezone a 150-acre tract from agricultural to industrial. This would allow them to develop a solar power generating plant there. Sam Creighton, the RAE project manager, had presented his case. He promised new jobs for the county, upgrades to the roads, and less pollution compared to the coal and gas-burning energy plants. Local residents had been voicing major opposition, citing concerns over the aesthetics and effects on local flora and wildlife. The board of supervisors had stalled, recommending a public forum to hear the opinions of county residents on such development.

Seems fair, thought Dr. Hardy. He looked out across the backyard and the bordering woods. The trees were in full foliage now, limiting his view of the lake to a snapshot look down the walking path. He held a strong appreciation of the natural beauty of this lake community. As he turned up his cup for the last swallow, he heard the drone of a distant outboard boat motor. The morning dew had nearly evaporated from the grass, and Dr. Hardy resolved himself to begin mowing the lawn.

It was one o'clock when Hardy took a lunch break. Lucy made them some sandwiches and she spoke as they ate. "I was thinking of going by Bill Bradson's when I go into town to check the mail. What do you think? Do you want to come?"

Bill was the local realtor they had contracted to sell their old home in town. They had leased it out for a couple of years, but it was currently vacant. They had placed it on the market three months ago. The house was built by Dr. Hardy's grandfather in 1935, using mules to haul the dirt up from the basement excavation. The Georgian-style home boasted a slate roof, copper gutters, and solid brick walls. Hardy was the third generation of his family to own it.

"Yeah. I can go with you. I can use a break."

Bradson Realty was on the same street as the post office. As they walked through the door, the realtor was leading a man into his office. The man looked familiar.

"Isn't that the Indian chief from the powwow?" Dr. Hardy asked Lucy.

"Yeah! I think it is," she said.

"Bill's in with a client now," said the receptionist. "He shouldn't be very long."

In Bradson's business office, the man spoke. "Mr. Bradson, I'm very interested in that land you are selling in the Beechwood area. I represent the Wyanoke Indians, and we have been looking for a larger site to establish a reservation. Our current place is only twenty-five acres."

"Mr. Heathcock, that acreage would be ideal. It's wooded and has 600 feet of frontage on the lake," said the realtor. Bill Bradson was about forty years old and kept his blond hair trimmed short.

"That's what we were thinking, too."

"Well, unfortunately, that property has just been placed under an option contract."

"An option?"

"Yeah. RAE, the solar power company, placed it under option

to purchase. They are waiting for the county to approve their project."

"That is bad news for us," said Heathcock. "How long is the option good for?"

"A year," said Bradson.

"I see." He paused pensively. "And, if their project does not get approved?"

"Well, they could still purchase it or, more likely, let their option expire. Then, it would be available to sell again."

"Hmm … Could you notify me first if they decide not to purchase this parcel?"

"Certainly! You'll be the first one I'll call before listing it." He stood up and offered his hand to the chief.

"Well, thank you, anyway." Mr. Heathcock shook Bill's hand.

As Mr. Heathcock walked out, Dr. Hardy gave him a cordial nod. The chief appeared to be disappointed.

"Dr. Hardy, Lucy," called out Bill Bradson. "Come on back here."

"Was he that Weyanoke Indian chief?" asked Lucy.

"Yeah," said Bradson. "He's looking for land for a reservation."

"Oh, really?" said Dr. Hardy.

"We were just checking on our house listing," said Lucy. "Any interest?"

"Well, we had two showings this month. No offers yet. However, I was asked how old the heat pumps are. Do you have that info?"

"Sure," said Dr. Hardy. "One is twenty years old and the newest is four."

"Okay. Great," said Bradson, making a note. "I'll let you know if we get any activity. It is a large house."

"Three stories and a basement," added Lucy.

"Yes, but it is eighty years old, too," he added.

CHAPTER 5

Dr. Hardy wrestled to get the winter cover off of his swimming pool. The plastic woven sheet was weighted by wet leaves that had slipped around the netted leaf cover. This was a disadvantage of having a pool bordering the forest. His phone vibrating in his holster startled him. He recognized the caller's number – the MEs office.

"Dr. Hardy here," he said.

"Hi. This is Investigator Bennett from the medical examiner's office. Are you available for a scene visit?"

"I guess so. Where is it?"

"Bracey. He was found dead at home. Last seen two weeks ago."

"Okay. It'll take me about forty-five minutes to get there." It was in the southeast corner of the county. The commute, scene time, and paperwork would take probably three hours to complete. He collected his ME bag and headed out.

The drive took him down Mitchell Road, along the river. The road shoulders, adjoining lawns, and ditches were picketed with small signs. They read: "No Solar Farms," "Keep the Countryside Green," and "RAE" in a cross-slashed red circle.

The neighborhood is voicing its opposition, thought Dr. Hardy. He wondered who had paid for the signage. Did the landowners pass the hat? Were they that seriously invested in this fight? There were also no signs for or against an Indian reservation. Maybe that was the sleeping dog in this debate.

The death scene address took him to a gated residential community. The dwellings consisted of a few houses but mostly mobile homes and camper-type trailers. They were tightly packed along the winding roads, somewhat tiered upon the rolling hills. The highlight of this conglomeration was a spectacular view of Lake Gaston as it sprawled out below the hills. The water's surface shimmered in the afternoon sunlight.

Such a beautiful place to die, thought Dr. Hardy. A county police car was parked in the narrow street at the scene address. He parked his Jeep on a 45-degree incline across the road from the scene. He set the parking brake before getting out. In front of the cabin stood Deputy Hudson, the young officer he had met at the vacant store death site.

"Dr. Hardy, I'm Sidney Hudson," he said.

"Yeah. Good to see you again."

"The decedent is Owen Lindsey. This is his residence." They walked onto the porch along the left side of the home up to the entrance. They stopped outside the door. "He's in the bedroom. Turn right and walk straight back. The bedroom is to the left." He looked at Dr. Hardy for a moment. "You'll have to go back alone. It's right bad. I had to throw up when we found him." Hudson's blank face told the story.

"Oh. So he's been dead for a while?"

"Last known contact was two weeks ago. He's known to drink heavily. There are empty bottles on the floor."

Hardy stalled briefly before opening the door. The first room he entered was a den or great room with a cathedral ceiling and large windows overlooking the lake. Stacks of boxes, papers, and electronic devices filled the room except for a narrow pathway to the far wall.

"A hoarder," Dr. Hardy said to himself, carefully choosing his footing as he traversed the maze. The stench of death had been noticeable when he opened the door but intensified as he approached the bedroom. He stopped at the doorway and set down his ME bag, hoping that the nylon fabric would absorb less of the fetid odor than it would if it was in closer proximity to the body.

After a few quick photos, he began examining the body. The man appeared Caucasian, but his skin was discolored brown. No rigor mortis was present, indicating he had died at least thirty-six hours before. The tissues of the face were swollen and distorted from lying face down. He attempted to draw a syringe of vitreous fluid, but the eyes had the consistency of an old banana, and no free fluid was obtained despite multiple stabs.

The decomposed skin pigment change was a brown color, making his race undeterminable. Hardy also needed to draw a blood sample. When he palpated the groin area, the outer skin slid around like that of a rotting tomato.

"Yuk!" came a voice from behind Dr. Hardy. He turned to see a curious Officer Hudson wearing a surgical type mask. "What's that for?"

"Blood for toxicologies, I hope," said Hardy. He made several passes but was only able to collect a 2-cc sample. "They request at least 10 cc for testing."

"Oh. That's neat."

"Who ID'd the body?"

"Oh, the other officers knew him. Apparently, he was an alcoholic." Even with the mask, Hudson appeared to be straining to stay in the room. "I'll be right outside," he added before a hasty departure. Curiosity had won out over nausea–but only temporarily.

Dr. Hardy retreated as well, with his camera and tiny blood specimen. He was met on the front porch by Detective Duffer.

"Fellers Funeral Home is having a funeral right now, and Drapers is refusing to come out. They're afraid they won't get paid for the pickup," said the detective.

Hudson stood beside the porch. With the likelihood that he'd need to wait indefinitely at the scene, he looked as green as a black man can.

"Too bad," said Hardy. "I'll fax in my report when I get home."

"Okay," said Duffer.

"Oh, I saw all the Indian names on the streets here. Was this old Indian territory?"

"Yeah. I believe so."

"It's not far from the proposed reservation, I see," said Dr. Hardy. "I ran into Chief Heathcock at the realtor's office this week."

"Oh yeah? Well, you know the body in Chase City was connected to it, don't you?"

"What do you mean?"

"Jon Griffin. He was planning to meet with the group organizing the reservation."

"And he died somewhat mysteriously," added Dr. Hardy.

"Yeah." Detective Duffer raised his eyebrows and said, "*natural causes.*"

CHAPTER 6

Mrs. Roark was a slender, eighty-four-year-old with pure white hair, sitting on an ER stretcher. She smiled pleasantly at Dr. Hardy. Her niece was at the bedside and relayed her history to the doctor.

"She has trouble explaining how she feels 'cause she's got a touch of dominia," she said.

Dr. Hardy recorded the word *dominia* on his note paper. He collected slang medical terms that he heard, mostly for entertainment. He dreamed of compiling a book of these words one day. "So what's going on with her today?"

"She has an e-regular heart, and I think it's causing her botheration."

"How is it bothering her?" He recorded *e-regular* heart and *botheration* in his notes.

"She's not getting around too well. Oh, and she takes that cool-a-den and had her R&R done last week."

He added to his word list *cool-a-den* and *R&R* for Coumadin and the blood test INR, the lab assessment of anticoagulation level. "Is she short of breath or having any chest pains?"

He could extract very little additional history from Mrs. Roark or her niece. He completed his exam and walked out to the work station. As he entered his computer orders, he said to the nurse, "I'm doing the arrhythmia protocol." He smiled as he added, "And, more importantly, I got five new words."

"Yeah. I'm sure you did!" she said, smiling back.

"Dr. Hardy," the unit secretary interrupted.

"Yes," he answered.

"There's a police officer out front that wants to talk to you."

"Okay. Send him back. I can talk to him before I start with the next patient."

Detective Duffer walked into the work station area of the ER carrying a brown paper bag.

"Hey, Bruce," said Dr. Hardy. "What's up?"

"Hi, Doc. Could you take a look at something for me? I need an expert opinion."

"Sure. What ya got?"

The detective held open the bag for Dr. Hardy to see inside. "We found these bones in the woods, and I don't think they're human. Can you verify that for me?"

"I think so," said Hardy. He picked up a vertebral bone that was narrow and elongated, not designed for upright weight bearing. "Not human." The next appeared to be a femur but was short and squatty and more arched than that of a person. "Nope, not human." Another specimen was the length of a human forearm, shaped like the radius bone. "Hmm," said Dr. Hardy. As he studied it closer, where the wrist joint would be, there were three articular grooves. "Closer, but still not human."

"Yeah. I suspected it was a deer or coyote."

"A deer, I suspect," said Dr. Hardy.

"And these," said Duffer, reaching into a lunch-sized paper bag. "I'm most suspicious of."

He handed Dr. Hardy four bones, about three inches long, that were straight. Hardy was startled by their appearance, resembling metatarsal foot bones. Something was a bit odd looking. They were a little more curved and heavy-set. He remembered seeing examples of bones like this at an ME training conference.

"I believe these are the bones of a bear!" he said.

"Okay. That would go along with some claws that we found there, too."

"Yeah. Where did you find these, anyway?"

"It was in the woods out on Mitchell Road. Thanks for your help, Doc."

"Sure. I can look at bones anytime. Who found them by the way?"

"Some engineers with that solar company."

"Oh? Why were they out there?"

"Seems they got a permit to set up a one-acre test site. A feasibility study or something."

"Really?"

"I think it's just to get their foot in the door. So they can test the waters, politically. Maybe to convince the landowners that it's nothing to be afraid of."

"I see. Well, thanks for the update."

"Sure. I'll see you later."

It was two weeks later when Dr. Hardy met Detective Duffer again. He had been called to a death scene off Mitchell Road. He met Duffer at the wooded roadside where his Crown Victoria was parked.

"You won't believe this one," he said to Dr. Hardy.

"What do you mean?"

They began walking into the woods. "The RAE engineers found some more bones. This time, it's a skull. Definitely human," said Duffer.

"How much of the body did you find?" asked Hardy.

"Just the skull, so far." They stopped behind the yellow crime scene tape that stretched around two trees and two wooden stakes. "...and some arrowheads."

Dr. Hardy's curiosity was stoked now. *A skull and arrowheads?* he thought. He took out his cell phone to shoot some photos of the scene. The leaf bed was thick in the area but had been brushed back to expose a brownish-colored skull. There were five white markers on the ground at the locations of stone-like structures, apparently projectile points.

"I got plenty of photos, too," said Duffer.

"Any clothing remnants found?" asked Hardy.

"No, but the skull looks pretty old, probably years old."

Dr. Hardy started a close examination of the "body," a skeletal cranium. It did appear to be decades old. There were no skin or hair remnants. There was no mandible and only a few upper teeth. No fracture marks or fragments were there that would imply that head trauma was a cause of death. There was, however, a crack along the left side that didn't look as aged as the skull.

"I think this crack in the parietal bone happened much more recently," he said. "The edges haven't dulled from the obvious age and exposure to the elements. I doubt it was related to the death. Probably from handling of the skull."

"I see," said the detective.

"The Richmond ME's office has an archaeological anthropologist that can help determine the body's age and race, as well as how long since the time of death."

"Okay. We'll bag it up along with the arrowheads. We'll be sifting the dirt around the skull to search for more bones."

"All right. I'll phone it in." Something seemed familiar about this to Hardy. Was it because of the bones that were found near here two weeks ago? "Wait a minute!" he said suddenly. He picked up his cell phone and accessed his photos. Scrolling through them, he stopped at the pictures taken at the powwow. "Ah ha!"

"What is it?" asked Duffer.

Dr. Hardy showed him his photo of the skull in the Indian museum gift shop. "I thought this skull looked familiar! Look." The picture showed the brownish skull, no jawbone, and a crack along the left side. "This is the skull from the Occoneechee Park museum display!"

"It sure is!" said Duffer. "What the hell?"

CHAPTER 7

Detective Duffer sat at his desk in the Mecklenburg County Sheriff's Office, sipping the last of his now tepid morning coffee. He was reviewing the theft report from the Occoneechee State Park gift shop robbery. The only items stolen were the old skull and some projectile points, nothing of immediate cash value. Easily sold items such as camping equipment and food products were left behind. The single security camera was aimed at the parking lot and had nothing useful recorded. The break-in was through the back entrance where the door window had been broken. There was an alarm system, but it had no battery backup and the power was shut off before the burglary.

Who would want these artifacts? he thought.

"Detective Duffer," interrupted Betsy, his secretary. She was standing in the doorway.

"Yes."

"There's someone here that Detective Wilborne sent over for you to see. A Tom Heathcock. He thought you might could help him."

"Okay. Send him in."

The visitor was in a gray suit with a white shirt. He was wearing a handmade necklace. "I'm Tom Heathcock, chief of the Wyanoke tribe," he stated.

"It's a pleasure," said Duffer. "What can we help you with?"

"I'm looking to get an injunction to stop the solar power

company from setting up tests on the property along Mitchell Road."

"An injunction? What basis do you have for this action?"

The chief's tone was serious. "There appears to be a sacred Wyanoke burial ground on that property."

"Like ... an historic site?" asked the detective.

"Yes, sir."

"I'm not familiar with any historic Indian ties there. Has this been documented?"

"Well, I'm submitting an application for it now. I've heard that some ancient remains have been discovered on the land."

Detective Duffer knew that the discovery of the skull had not been made public. He sensed something suspicious going on here. "We did investigate some bones found there about two weeks ago, but they were not human. And they were not very old." This was indeed true.

"Oh, I see," replied Heathcock. He did not seem convinced by the statement.

"I'd recommend that you get your documentation submitted to designate it as an historic site, first. Then, we'll see what we can do to get that court order."

"Okay. I just hope I can get this done before it's too late. Thank you, Detective."

"Sure. And good luck." He had a sudden after thought. "Oh, do you have a card or phone number?"

"Yes, of course." He handed Duffer his card.

"Thanks. And, Chief. I'm just curious. What are those things strung on your necklace?"

"These?" He held up one of the brown, comma-shaped objects. "They are bear's claws. Native heritage."

"Oh, I see. That's neat. Thanks!"

"Tribal belief is that some animal spirits possess supernatural powers. Just be mindful of this if our burial ground is violated."

"Thanks, Chief. I'll keep that in mind."

There had been bear's bones and claws recovered from the site a few weeks ago. The chief's allusion to a tribal burial ground and wearing a bear-claw necklace seemed a bit too coincidental. He placed his card with the theft report. *He's a person of interest in this robbery,* he thought. Holding down the page button on his desk phone, he said, "Betsy."

"Yes, sir?" she answered.

"Can you get me the Richmond ME's office, please?"

"Sure." After a brief pause, she called back, "ME's office on line two."

"Thanks, Betsy … Hi, Detective Duffer here. Can I speak to someone about the skull we sent you from Mecklenburg County?"

"Okay. That's Investigator Bennett. I'll transfer you."

"Investigator Bennett," said a female voice.

"Hello. This is Detective Duffer from Mecklenburg County. I was calling to check on the examination of the skull we sent up there."

"Oh, yeah. We had the Virginia Museum anthropologist, Carl Wheatherlee, examine it. He remembered it from when he processed it for the park. Probably early 1900s and African American race."

"Okay. Any chance it is American Indian? It was in an Indian display."

"Possibly. He did say there was a lot of interracial pairing between blacks and Native Americans during that time."

"All right. Thanks for your info."

"Sure. You should have the report this week."

So, the skull was definitely the one that was stolen. The race was, at most, only partially Native American. Why was it found off Mitchell Road, and how did Chief Heathcock know about it?

CHAPTER 8

A white pickup truck turned into the woods off Mitchell Road. The license plate read "HUNTR," and the rear window had a silhouette deer head emblem. It stopped between two wooden markers tagged with pink ribbons. Two young men got out of the truck and began inspecting the trees. They appeared to be about twenty years old.

"How about this oak?" said the driver. He was wearing jeans and a Chevrolet T-shirt. His companion wore a Tractor Supply baseball-type cap and a Virginia Beach T-shirt.

"Well, Rodney, I was hoping to put a platform up there, and it doesn't have a cluster of limbs like we need."

"Okay. How about this sweet gum, Phillip?" He pointed to a tree with a trunk that was two and a half to three feet across.

"Yeah. That'll do. Let's get the ladder and unload some wood."

Piled in the back of the pickup were ten two-by-fours, two sheets of plywood, and a ladder.

"So, you want to be up about ten to twelve feet above the ground?" asked Rodney.

"Yeah. Just above that second level of limbs."

Phillip was slimmer than Rodney, and he climbed the ladder to the limbs that were five to six inches thick. Rodney passed him up four two-by-fours that he arranged and nailed to the tree. He next set the other studs in a parallel pattern eight feet across to support the plywood flooring. Rodney slid the plywood panels up along the ladder for Phillip to set in place.

"Hey. Can you get me the reciprocating saw?" he asked Rodney. "I need to cut some notches to fit the floor against the trunk and a limb or two."

"Okay." Rodney stepped up on the ladder a few steps to hand him the battery-powered saw. "Here you go."

"Thanks."

While Phillip customized his tree deck, Rodney hammered a sign post into the ground near the truck. Phillip came down from the tree and looked up to admire his carpentry work.

"I guess we're set," he said. "I never thought this is how I'd spend summer break."

"Yeah. Virginia Tech will be a breeze after staying out here. Oh, here's your roof." He grinned, handing Phillip a folded tarp.

"Thanks," said Phillip sarcastically. "You know, we need a rope or something to send up supplies. What do you think?"

"I heard that." Rodney had been up and down the ladder handing up wood, nails, and tools. "Hey! I've got it! There's something in Granddaddy Jenkins's old barn. I'll bring it out."

"Okay. Did you post the notice?"

"Oh, not yet." Rodney got a paper note in a clear plastic cover and the staple gun from the front seat of the pickup truck. He stapled the notice to the sign post he had erected. Phillip read the sign aloud.

"Petition by Mecklenburg Forest Preservation to prohibit destruction of woodland habitat."

"Sounds official enough," said Rodney. "I'll see you this evening with supper."

"Okay. Thanks, Rodney."

"Oh, I almost forgot." He reached over into the truck bed. "Here's your master bathroom!"

He handed Phillip a shovel and slid a roll of toilet paper onto the handle.

CHAPTER 9

Monday morning a stout man appearing to be about forty came into the sheriff's office. He wore a dress shirt and had the appearance of an office worker. The top of his head was balding. He seemed impatient and a little agitated.

"Can I help you?" asked the lady at the reception desk.

"Yes! I need to speak to someone about trespassers at the RAE solar test site!"

"Okay. I'll get an officer to speak with you, sir."

It was only minutes before Carl Wilborne opened the entrance door. He stood eight inches taller than the plaintiff.

"Come on back, sir. I'm Detective Wilborne. We'll see what we can do."

"Thanks," he replied. As they walked into the hallway, he continued, "I'm Sam Creighton, project manager for RAE."

"The solar energy company?"

"Yeah. We've got trespassers on our test site."

"Oh, yeah? Let's see if Detective Duffer is in. He's working a case on that property already."

"Okay."

They walked into the secretaries' station.

"Betsy, is Duffer in? We need to talk with him," said Wilborne.

"Yes. He just refilled his coffee." She showed them over to his office cubicle.

"Dennis," said Wilborne, "this is Sam Creighton with the

RAE solar power company. He's having problems at the Mitchell Road site."

"Oh, yeah? What's up?" asked Duffer.

"There's trespassers, squatters, on the test site!" said Creighton.

"Squatters? That's odd," said Duffer. "I didn't know that property had been sold."

"Well, not yet. We have an option on it and a permit for a pilot test site."

"Okay," said Duffer.

"They had this posted there." Creighton handed Duffer a plastic-covered paper with holes in the corners. Duffer studied it briefly and handed it to Wilborne.

"So, this is a petition filed with the county by Mecklenburg Forest Preservation. I haven't heard of them before. Nevertheless, you can't proceed at that site until the judge rules on this petition," said Duffer.

"But there's people camped out there in a tree house!"

"Let me check the docket," said Duffer. He sat down at his desk computer and worked the screen. "It seems the judge has this scheduled for two weeks from now."

"Two weeks?" exclaimed Creighton. "We scheduled to have the site cleared this week. We have a permit for a one-acre test field."

"I'm afraid you'll have to wait until the judge rules on this," said Wilborne.

"We can't start clearing the site?"

"No. Not yet," said Duffer.

"What about the trespassers?"

"Well, you're not the owner of the property. With the option and a permit for usage, you would be considered a tenant. You could charge someone for trespassing," said Wilborne.

"But," added Duffer, "you can't start work there until the case is ruled on anyway. And, do you want any negative publicity now? Kicking local environmentalists out of the woods?" Duffer knew the test site was just a ploy to show the public how safe and innocuous solar fields were.

"Yeah," said Creighton, thoughtfully. "Maybe you're right."

"Besides," said Wilborne. "They may get tired, give up, and go home."

"We'll ride by there a couple of times a day," said Duffer. "Just to keep tabs on the protesters."

"Well, okay."

"Oh. If you have any environmental safety data, you might want to get it together for the judge," added Duffer.

"Yeah. Right," he said, unconvincingly. "Thank you, Officers."

Detective Wilborne escorted Mr. Creighton out of the sheriff's office and returned to Duffer's office.

"I'll drive out there and take a look-see at the protesters," he said.

"Okay. Let me know what you find," said Duffer.

"Sure thing."

About an hour later, Wilborne returned to the sheriff's office where Duffer was still at work.

"The protesters were easy to find," he said to Duffer.

"Yeah?"

"Yeah. There were two pickups parked there and another vehicle. That reporter, Mark Malone, was writing an article on the protest. College kids, the Merit and Jenkins boys, I think."

"Any disorderly activity?"

"No. It's fairly organized and civil. They have their petition posted and a platform set up in a tree."

"Sounds pretty benign to me. We'll just keep an eye on them anyway," said Duffer.

Phillip Merit sat alone in his tree perch. He had just eaten a can of stew he had heated on a propane camping burner. It wasn't haute cuisine, but the view was unbeatable. From his height, he could see some of the surface of Lake Gaston, the setting sun shooting fiery red reflections from the waves. A gentle breeze through the tree shade promised some reprieve from the oppressive July heat. Three solar lights lit up as the daylight died out. The lights by the latrine and the ladder were quite useful in the woods at night. Phillip smiled at the irony of solar-charged lights used to protest a solar power farm. Without electricity, his cell phone charger also drew its power from the sun.

The tree frogs filled the air with their chirping-like sounds that were most intense during the early night. During the evening serenade, he heard a low-pitched sound start up. It was a thumping noise, like a drum. He checked his phone to be sure it wasn't playing music. The rhythm continued. *Pum-pum-pump, pum-pum-pump. That's strange,* he thought. From Mitchell Road, about one hundred yards away, the drone of an occasional passing car interrupted his nights. Suddenly, headlights flickered through the tree leaves. There arose a particularly bright light that grew more intense, and he heard an automobile just below his roost.

"Hey! Tarzan! Are you up there?" called a female voice. He immediately knew his girlfriend's voice.

"Sandra. What are you doing here?"

"Thought you might want some company. Can I come up?"

"Sure. Be careful though."

Sandra was smallish, about five foot four, with chestnut hair in a ponytail. She had on a purple JMU T-shirt and white shorts.

"I've got a couple beers here." She held up a six-pack of Natural Lights.

"Great. Put 'em in the lift." He lowered a rope with a net-like sling on the end. It was the device Rodney had rigged up for him from an old barn hoist. The pulley was mounted to a boom hinged on the trunk and could swing out from the platform. She put the beer on the lift and climbed up.

"Pretty neat dumb waiter," she said, crawling onto the deck.

"Yeah. It's great." He pulled out a beer. "Hey, these are cold! That's a luxury out here." He opened the can, handed it to Sandra, and grabbed another one for himself. As they drank the beers, Phillip shared his mosquito repellent. "Here, let me rub some on your back." He reached under her T-shirt to massage in the lotion and discovered that she was not wearing a bra. "So, the puppies are running free, huh?"

She smiled and replied, "Yeah."

Phillip hugged her, keeping his hands underneath her shirt, feeling the soft skin of her back. He kissed her passionately, sliding his hands onto her breasts. She pressed against him and sighed softly. As their cuddling intensified, she suddenly paused and spoke.

"I'm afraid we might fall out of this tree."

"Well, I have an idea," said Phillip. "You see, my mind wanders up here, alone … for hours."

"What do you mean?"

He grabbed the pulley lift arm and swung it around on the hinge so it was overlying the deck. The sling was nylon rope netting like a hammock. He spread it open with his hands and grinned.

"I can hold you up in the lift." He bobbed the sling up and down.

"Oh," she said. "Do you think it will hold me up?"

"It has a 350-pound capacity. It could hold *both* of us up together."

He unrolled his foam mattress pad and they sat down on it. She straddled his lap, facing him. Phillip embraced her, sliding his hands along her bare back. As they kissed, he sensed her arousal. Their kissing intensified as he cupped her breasts in his hands. She gave a subdued sigh. He felt that her nipples had become firm, and her hands groped his neck and scalp.

"It seems to be getting a bit warmer now," he said as he pulled her shirt up over her light brown hair.

"Yes. I believe so," she said and giggled as she removed his shirt as well.

He pulled her against his torso, feeling the warmth of her body. As he kissed her, he felt her press her pelvis against him. This brought his growing erection to full attention.

She stood up over him and pulled down her shorts and panties together. Pulling the sling up behind her, she sat back in it like a swing. As she positioned herself in a squatting position, she handed the lift rope to Phillip.

"You're in charge, babe," she said with an impish smile. He pulled in on the line and she rose slightly, suspended in the lift. Her hand touched his firm organ, guiding it to her crotch. He slowly lowered her, feeling her warmth engulf him.

"Oh! That's great!" he said. As he tugged and released tension on the rope, Sandra slid up and down on him. Phillip's pelvis reflexively followed the waves of her movements. His arousal intensified, and she seemed to sense it. Just as he was reaching a climax, she spun around like she was on a swivel stool.

"Helicopter!" she cried out.

"A-a-a-ah!" he responded as pulsations of orgasm flowed through him. He released the rope, and she melted down onto him.

"That was a fun ride," she said.

"Yeah. It was sensational! Are we in the mile-high club now?"

"Well, technically, the *helicopter* doesn't count as the mile-high club."

"I'll take the treetop swingers club any day."

CHAPTER 10

It was a sultry July day that found Dr. Hardy working in the field in front of his house. The air felt thick from the humidity, making his sweaty clothing cling to his body. He was piling tree limbs over stumps, preparing them to burn. The plan was to make the cut-over timber field into a pasture. Thick brush growth in the lower part of the four-acre lot covered a wet marshy area. This was the biggest obstacle in the process. The fencing crew had helped rough grade the field with a Bobcat bucket tractor but ended up getting stuck in the muddy bottom. After being pulled out, the driver said that area needed heavier equipment with metal treads to clear.

The moisture seemed to seep out from the ground, lending to growth of thick, stalky marsh grass and a few cattails. Hardy pulled on some tree branches and stump roots embedded in the mud. He was trying to locate a stream or creek bed to dig out for drainage. Several spots seemed to trickle fluid. Finally, he discovered a strong, steady flow of water at the base of a rock pile. He dug away some of the mud with his grubbing hoe, and the water force was enough to wash away the muddy water, leaving a clear sparkling stream.

"Yes, a spring!" he said. Digging a ditch from here could channel the water and help drain the bog. Moreover, the clear spring water would be an excellent water source for the horses. It would surely beat hauling pails of water out daily.

The sound of a vehicle in the gravel driveway made Hardy look up. He saw his wife's pickup truck approaching the house. Feeling drained from working in the heat, he thought this might be a good time for a lunch break. He followed her through the garage door into the house.

"You want some lunch?" she asked.

"Yeah. I need some water first though." The cool indoor air was welcoming. "I found the main spring in the pasture."

"Oh. Is that good?"

"Yeah. Maybe we can dig a little pond from the spring for the horses to drink from."

"Can you do that yourself?" she asked.

"No. We'll need a bulldozer. I've heard Buck Warren does reasonable work. Maybe we should give him a call."

"Sounds good."

Lucy had put the morning mail on the kitchen island. He grabbed the local *News Progress* to look through while he rehydrated.

"Tree Sitters Block the Sun," he read aloud.

"What?" said Lucy.

"It seems RAE got a permit for a test site on the Mitchell Road land. Apparently, a group, Mecklenburg Forest Preservation, or MFP, got a petition filed to delay the construction."

"So, what's going to happen there?"

"I don't know. It says the judge felt there was insufficient environmental safety data and deferred making a ruling for another two weeks. I guess a decision would establish a precedent, and he wanted to be sure."

"That makes sense. Who owns that land anyway?" She was assembling some sandwiches.

"I think it was inherited by three sisters. Thompsons, I think. Another roadblock in the sale." He turned the page of the newspaper. "Oh. Bluegrass in Boydton is this Saturday. You wanna go?"

"Yeah, maybe." She placed his sandwich on a paper plate. "Do you want this heated?"

"No! I've had a plenty of heat!" he replied. "Thanks."

CHAPTER 11

The Boyd Tavern was established in 1785 by the founding family of Boydton. It had served as a tavern, an inn, a courthouse, and the local poll. The old train depot was three blocks away. Located on the block adjacent to the county courthouse, it was still the hub of the town. Its front porch served as the stage for the Bluegrass in Boydton bands. The town of five hundred residents was alive with food and beverage booths, including a beer truck. Folding chairs crowded the street facing the tavern.

"Wow," said Dr. Hardy. "I think there's more than the population of Boydton here!" He and Lucy walked past the beer station and down to the food vendors. "You want a baloney burger?" A local favorite at ball games and fairs, the sandwich was a thick slice of baloney fried with onions and peppers. None of these were items that Lucy would eat.

"No thanks," wrinkling her nose. "I'll stick with the barbecue plate."

They carried their food to the front lawn of the courthouse. Several musicians were gathered under a large oak tree and were playing enthusiastically. There was a bass fiddle, mandolin, banjo, steel guitar, and a fiddle. Several acoustic guitars were also in the assembly.

"I think this is just a jam session," said Dr. Hardy as they approached.

"It's definitely bluegrass," said Lucy.

They watched as the pickup ensemble played a few songs, some musicians trading instruments between numbers. Then, they started packing up as the featured show was due to begin.

"Grab me a beer, and I'll get the chairs from the truck," said Hardy. He handed Lucy some cash.

"Okay."

They met back in the street and sat in the folding chairs.

"Oh, it's Buggs Island Bluegrass!" said Hardy, recognizing the local band. "That's Bruce Duffer's band."

"Oh, yeah. They're good!"

In the early evening sunlight they could see many familiar faces in the crowd. People ate and drank during the performance. The fast-picking banjo and fiddle set the bluegrass beat while the drums, guitar, and bass added the richness. Bruce Duffer manned the guitar as well as sang some of the songs.

After their performance, the band members packed up their instruments and began milling about the crowd. Bruce Duffer drifted over to where Dr. Hardy and Lucy were sitting. Duffer was drinking from a water bottle. Dr. Hardy had never seen him drink a beer, on or off duty.

"Doc," said Duffer. "You know, you were right about that skull."

"The one from Occoneechee Park?"

"Yeah. It was the stolen one. It's African American, possibly Native American mix."

"That sure is odd," said Hardy.

"Yeah, it is. I think it may have something to do with the Indians wanting that land for a reservation. No proof of that, though."

"That's crazy. And, I read there's tree sitters out there too," said Hardy.

"Yeah. The solar power company wants that land too."

"Sounds like a hillbilly feud from one of your bluegrass songs!"

"Yeah. It does!"

"Well, y'all were awesome tonight with that bluegrass!" said Lucy.

"We thoroughly enjoyed it," added Hardy.

"Thanks. It's a lot of fun. Y'all take care. I'll see you around."

"Okay. You too," said Hardy.

CHAPTER 12

Detective Duffer always felt that the general district courtroom resembled a small church. The bench seats were like pews on either side of a central aisle. Today there were fifteen people from Mecklenburg Forest Preservation filling the benches facing the judge's pulpit. They anxiously awaited the ruling on their petition. Judge Logan weeded through the tenant disputes and debt warrants before reaching their case.

"Mecklenburg Forest Preservation versus Radiant Acquired Energy," he announced.

Two spokespersons from MFP stood up and the female stated, "Mecklenburg Forest Preservation is here, Your Honor."

Sam Creighton rose from a seat to the right side. He held a folder of papers under his arm. "RAE here, Your Honor."

"So, Mecklenburg Forest, please state the grounds upon which you base your charges against RAE."

"Your Honor," said the female, "I'm Evelyn Merit, representing MFP." She was middle-aged with shoulder-length brown hair that had a slight wave to it. Her business attire gave her a professional look. She worked as a legal assistant. "Solar fields strip properties of trees, bushes, and even grass. A single acre of forest can have five hundred trees on it. Not only are they a green source of oxygen, but they provide habitats for wildlife, including game animals. Deer, rabbits, turkeys, and even bears live there. Fenced-in solar fields will displace these animals and disrupt migration patterns as well. Not in the least, the natural beauty of wooded areas form the scenic shoreline of Lake Gaston. Camping and other outdoor and water recreation activities are a basis of our local economy."

"I see. Do you have evidence or estimates of the damages the solar field would incur?" asked the judge.

There was a pause before Ms. Merit responded. "No, sir. Nothing specific."

"Okay. Thank you for your concerns." The judge addressed Mr. Creighton. "So, RAE, do you have a response to these claims?"

"Yes, Your Honor. Mecklenburg County has about 435,000 acres, including over half of a 50,000-acre lake. In addition to the lake, there are 10,078 acres of parks and wildlife preserves. It has many agricultural and forest acres as well. Our test site is just a one-acre lot. Our entire project, if zoning approves it, would be only 300 acres. The Wal-Mart parking lot is 8 acres.

"The alternative to our solar farm would be another fossil-fuel-burning power plant. This could cover 20 acres, create air pollution, and release carbon dioxide that is responsible for global warming.

"As for the aesthetics, there will be a buffer zone of evergreen trees along the perimeter. If one didn't already know it was there, the solar farm would be inconspicuous."

Sam Creighton had definitely come prepared. Detective Duffer had noted that the judge had listened studiously. He then spoke. "And, what about this test site?"

"It's to establish the amount of solar energy potential at this location. It will also show how safe this project would be. Other solar farms of up to 300 acres have shown no effects on the game kills in those counties." He passed a sheet of paper to the clerk for the judge to review. "Any fields erected on privately purchased lands were not accessible to the general public for recreational activities anyway. As a benefit, most communities with solar-generation panels demonstrate that they are conservative but progressive and have a power grid to attract businesses."

The judge took little time before speaking. "I see no evidence that indicates a solar energy test site or even an entire farm poses any significant environmental or economic danger to Mecklenburg County. Radiant Acquired Energy, you may proceed with your proposed land development. The injunction is denied."

"Thank you, Your Honor," said Mr. Creighton. There arose some disgruntled mumbling amongst the MFP supporters. As the chatter grew louder, the judge pounded down with his gravel.

"Order!" he exclaimed. "Order!"

The courtroom suddenly grew quiet. Sam Creighton turned and began walking up the aisle to the back courtroom exit. He appeared calm and composed to Duffer. There was no evidence of gloating over his victory. Duffer watched as Creighton passed by. In the rear of the courtroom, he took notice of a man who was standing back there. It was Chief Heathcock. It was odd that Duffer had not noticed him there earlier. Their gazes locked for a moment. Then, Heathcock turned and quietly walked out.

I guess he has a vested interest in that property too, he thought. Next, he would need to send out a deputy to evict the tree sitters. He exited the courtroom and headed to his office. In the hallway of the sheriff's office, he ran into Detective Wilborne.

"Hey, Carl," he said. "You very busy now?"

"Not bad. What's up?" said Wilborne.

"Do you remember the tree sitters on Mitchell Road?"

"Yeah."

"Well, the judge okayed the property development, and they have to vacate the lot now."

"Oh? Okay. I can do that."

"Great. Do you need any assistance?"

"No. Should be a piece of cake."

"Okay. Thanks, man!"

About half an hour later, Duffer's cell phone rang. He saw Wilborne's number on the screen.

"Hello," said Duffer.

"Bruce. We got a problem out here on Mitchell Road," said Wilborne. His tone was serious.

"What do you mean?"

"You need to get out here. The tree squatter is missing. Looks like some fishy stuff happened out here."

"I'm on the way."

If Carl Wilborne asked him to come, something had gone down. He rushed out to the scene. He found the squatter's site where Wilborne's police cruiser was parked. Beside it was a white pickup truck with a "HUNTR" license plate. Wilborne was standing beside a stout young man.

"Bruce, this is Rodney Jenkins." Duffer gave Jenkins a nod. "His buddy, Phillip Merit, was sitting in this tree. Phillip's mother is with the MFP petitioners. When she got the verdict, she called him but didn't get an answer. So, she asked Rodney to come pick him up."

"Okay," acknowledged Duffer.

"When I got here, sir, Phillip was gone," said Rodney. "I've been bringing him food and clothes and all. But today, he's not here!"

"His cell phone was lying on the ground over there," Wilborne said, gesturing under the tree. "But, this is the weirdest thing. Take a look at this." He pointed to a wooden rod extending out from the trunk of the tree. "This is an arrow in the tree!"

The arrow had a stone arrowhead and real feathers in the quill. It appeared handmade, Native American style.

"It looks like an authentic Indian arrow!" said Duffer.

"That's what I thought too."

"Okay. This has become a crime scene. Tape it off, keep everyone out, and let's start collecting evidence."

CHAPTER 13

A gray SUV roared up to the Mitchell Road site, and the female driver jumped out. Detective Duffer recognized her as Evelyn Merit, from the MFP. She had a look of panic as she rushed over to him.

"Phillip!" she cried out. "Have you found my child, Phillip, yet?" she pleaded.

"Ms. Merit, I'm Detective Duffer," he said. "We're doing all we can now to find your son." In his gloved hand, he was holding her son's cell phone in a clear plastic evidence bag. She looked at it and began to cry.

"Oh no! What's happened? My poor baby!"

"Ms. Merit, when did you last see your son?"

"He texted me last night. He wished me luck in court today. Oh my god! Did I do this to him? He was doing this for me. For the forest preservation." She held her hand over her mouth and continued to cry.

Standing behind Duffer, Wilborne was also gloved and was putting the arrow in a brown paper bag.

"Oh my God! Was he shot?"

"Ma'am, we're looking into every possibility. Right now, we know he's been missing less than twenty-four hours. When was it you last contacted Phillip?" He was trying to use rational thinking to dampen her hysteria.

"Well . . . about ten last night. That's when he texted me. But nothing today."

"Yeah. Same with me," said Rodney. He was standing near the detectives. "We texted last night. He didn't respond to my texts today either."

"Under these circumstances," said Duffer, "we won't wait the usual twenty-four hours. We'll focus our full attention on this case."

"Thank you, Detective."

"You're welcome, Ms. Merit."

Rodney interjected the conversation again. "Detective, Phillip told me it was eerie at night. He claims he heard thumping sounds a couple of nights—like Indian drums. And some nights he heard animals howling and something rustling in the bushes around the tree."

"Well, there are coyotes around here," said Duffer.

"Yeah. He knew that. But this sounded like a large animal, maybe a bear."

"Oh my God!" said Ms. Merit.

Duffer hoped his next request would not alarm Ms. Merit. "Oh, can you get me a recent photo of Phillip? And maybe a personal item that might have some of his DNA?"

"Yes. I can bring it by the sheriff's office today."

"That would be great. I'll see you there."

Detective Duffer returned to the office after completing his sweep for clues. He hadn't shared with Ms. Merit the findings he had discovered in the tree stand. There were several blood smears that they had swabbed for typing and DNA. Additionally, there was what he was studying in a clear plastic evidence bag. It was a small cluster of hair follicles attached to a sliver of skin, no larger than a pencil eraser. An Indian arrow and this scalp shaving aroused memories of the serial killer case from a couple of years ago. In that case, the murderer had scalped his victims. A cool chill spread through his body.

The detective couldn't shake the feeling that Chief Heathcock was somehow involved in this. How had he known about the bogus Indian skeletal remains? Was his desire for the Mitchell Road place strong enough to lead to this abduction or worse? Could those sounds that Phillip had heard have really been Indian drums?

Duffer's cell phone rang. It was his son, Nick. "Hello, Nick," he said.

"Hey, Dad." Nick lived in Petersburg where he worked at the fire station.

"What's up?" His son never called him at work.

"Something's come up. Do you know about the wildfires in California?" Duffer had seen the news coverage over the past week. There had already been two deaths among the forest firefighters. He had an ominous feeling, since Nick was a full-time fireman in the city.

"Yeah. I've seen it in the news."

"Well, I've volunteered to go out there and help."

"What?"

"I've joined up with a volunteer group, and we're flying out West tomorrow."

"Son, you know that's very dangerous. Men have already died fighting that fire."

"Yeah. So they need all the help they can get. I want to help out."

"Couldn't you just send them a donation or something?" Duffer knew he was wasting his breath trying to convince Nick to abandon this crusade. His son was headstrong and altruistic, traits he had passed down to him.

"I gotta do this, Dad."

"Yeah. I know. I had hoped not though." There was a brief heavy silence. "Be careful, Son. I love you."

"Yeah. Me too."

CHAPTER 14

Yellow flames darted up from the burning pile of stumps and roots. Dr. Hardy was tending the fire with a stick cut from a sapling. It was September, the last days of summer by the calendar. The weather was still hot and humid, making the heat of the brush fire feel more intense. He was burning off some brush and weeds he had cleared from the pasture area and piled on a large stump. Buck Warren was scheduled to start bulldozing the marsh area in the bottom in the morning. The plan was to form several drainage ditches that would run together to form a stream. The major spring was to have a small pond dug out over it for pooling of drinking water.

The horses will never appreciate all that we've done to prepare this pasture, he thought. A patient of his had once told him that horses were "expensive yard ornaments." He had spoken the truth.

Hardy took a break for supper. A cold beer made a refreshing appetizer. Lucy had prepared grilled tuna steaks and blue-cheese-topped sweet potatoes. They sat down and blessed the meal.

"Do you want to go to church tomorrow?" asked Lucy.

"Yeah. That might be nice since I'm not working this weekend."

"Okay. I'll have to wash my hair," said Lucy.

"Me too. I smell like I've been in the fires of hell already."

She wrinkled her nose. "Yes, you do!"

The following day, Dr. Hardy and Lucy drove into town for church. It was an old brick building with majestic twelve-foot-tall windows along each side. It was built in 1873, but the church was founded by Randolph Macon College of Boydton in the 1830s. It was warming up already by the time of the service. Dr. Hardy worked every other weekend, and they didn't attend every Sunday that he was off. This was a treat for them. Despite any discord that might exist between church members, worshiping was a common ground, a goodness they could share.

After the service they mingled with other attendees in the foyer and at the area in front of the entrance steps. Dr. Hardy approached Bruce Duffer and spoke.

"Hey, Bruce. Haven't found any more bones, have you?"

"Nope. Not exactly." Duffer glanced around them and leaned in, speaking softly. "Maybe another scalp, though."

"What?" Hardy was aghast. He remembered the scalping deaths in a serial killer case they had investigated a couple of years ago.

"Well, a skin fragment with hair attached. The tree sitter is mysteriously missing. Looks like there may have been foul play."

"I know what it reminds me of," said Hardy.

"Yeah. Me too. We'll keep working it."

"Okay. Take care."

It was only two days before Dr. Hardy and Detective Duffer were joined again by the call of duty. Hardy had been dispatched to a death scene along Interstate 85, near Bracey. It was about 3:00 PM, a sunny day with only a few, cotton-ball clouds spotting the sky. Hardy had driven along the back roads before turning south on the interstate. On the right shoulder, about a mile past the Bracey exit, was a silver-colored sedan and a county police cruiser. He parked his Jeep a respectful distance behind the other vehicles. Duffer was holding a camera and approached him on foot with Carl Wilborne close behind him.

"Hey, Doc," said Duffer. "We found a body down here and

think he belongs to this abandoned vehicle. Someone reported it on the roadside this morning."

"It's registered to a Sadiq Stachys of Kittrell, North Carolina," said Wilborne. "Oddly enough, his wife was found murdered yesterday."

"Oh, yeah?" said Hardy. This was an awful scenario. "You think it's a murder-suicide?"

"That's our assumption at this point," said Duffer. "We saw a path through the reeds." He pointed to the bank of the lake. Hardy saw no obvious tract through the tall stalks crowding the shoreline. He walked down to the water's edge and looked out over the surface. He saw no signs of a corpse.

"It's that spot over there, where the ripples ring out from," said Duffer. He pointed off to the left. An object just below the surface slowly bobbed up and down, breaking the surface slightly.

"Is it very deep there?" Hardy asked.

"Probably eight to ten feet." That sounded deep enough to drown for a nonswimmer. "We have a boat at the steel bridge that we can use to reach him. That's the closest launch ramp."

"Okay. I'll meet you there."

Although the boat was only two miles upstream, it was over six miles by land. Hardy found the open skiff vessel and boarded it with the two detectives. The cruise back to the death scene slowly passed by the Mitchell Road property, off the port side. From the wooded land arose a dense green horizon, almost majestic. This natural beauty showed no signs of the raging dispute that was ensuing over it. As they approached the interstate bridge, the boat slowed down and the motor shut off.

"We have to wait for the dive team," said Duffer. Hardy noticed that a brown sheriff's van was positioned on the shoulder of the road. "They have to photograph the body as it's positioned in the water. Then we can load him up so you can do your exam."

"Okay. Sure."

"The North Carolina police found his wife in their mobile

home. She appeared to have been struck in the head, and the home had been set on fire," said Duffer.

"Oh my God!" said Hardy.

"Seems he had won $50,000 in the lottery. I guess it brought their marital problems to a head."

"The curse of the lottery," said Wilborne.

"Oh. And his relatives said he could not swim."

"That's important information," said Hardy.

The two divers surfaced beside the boat.

"It's a bit muddy, but we got the photos," said a diver. "You ready to load him up?"

"Sure," said Duffer. He and Wilborne unfolded a white mesh net and tossed it into the lake. The divers wrapped the body and floated it alongside the boat. Everyone assisted in wrestling the heavy catch into the boat. The divers headed back to shore as Hardy began assessing the decedent.

The man was middle-aged, about 180 pounds wet-weight. He wore a T-shirt and jeans with apparently dark-complexioned skin. He was in a fetal-like position with rigor mortis in his arms and legs.

"Rigor is still present. He's been dead less than seventy-two hours," said Hardy.

"Yeah. We think last evening," said Duffer.

Hardy found no fatal wounds or obvious fractures.

"He needs an autopsy."

"Yeah. Tanner's Funeral Home will meet us at the boat ramp," said Duffer.

Wilborne and Duffer spread a sheet over the body and began their voyage upstream.

Once at the launch site, Dr. Hardy disembarked. He turned to the officers and said, "I guess the lottery was actually *bad* luck for them."

"Yeah. Except maybe for his estate," said Duffer.

CHAPTER 15

Detective Bruce Duffer poured himself a cup of coffee from the pot in the sheriff's department lounge. He was feeling a bit groggy this morning. This was likely due to watching the late-night news, reporting on the California wildfires. They were still not controlled, and the winds were strong. Sitting at his desk, he removed his glasses and rubbed his eyes. He was about halfway through his cup of coffee when Betsy brought him the morning mail.

"Thanks," he mumbled and began sifting through the envelopes. The Richmond forensic lab letter caught his attention. DNA testing was now in such demand that results often took six weeks to obtain. Due to the circumstances of this missing person, he had requested that it be high priority. Results in three days were still surprising. He quickly opened it up and eagerly scanned the report. It was of little surprise that the hair and skin from the scene were indeed those of Phillip Merit.

He pressed his speaker phone. "Betsy. Can you get me the phone number of Tom Heathcock, please?"

"Sure. Right away."

Chief Heathcock accepted the detective's request to come in for a chat. He was available that afternoon. When he arrived, Duffer led him into the conference room, and they sat at the table. He planned to press him and possibly elicit some clue.

"Chief Heathcock, I appreciate you coming in and meeting with me," the detective began.

"Certainly, Detective. I'll do anything I can to help."

"You know of the judge's decision on the solar farm petition, I guess."

"Yes. I'm aware of the ruling. It was not as my people had hoped for." That had been obvious to Duffer, having seen his reaction in the courtroom.

"Well, the night before the court case, the tree-sitter protester went missing. It appears that he was kidnapped or worse."

"I'm sorry to hear that. He was actually an ally to our cause."

He appeared sincere to Duffer. The sitter had delayed RAE from accessing the property for several weeks. However, there *was* Indian evidence that was found. "I have to ask you, anyway," said Duffer. "Where were you four days ago?"

"Me? I was at a meeting in DC. We have our political action committees like everyone else."

His composure was solid. "I returned the morning of the petition ruling."

"I see," said the detective. After a pensive pause, he continued. "Do you know of any other person or parties that have shown interests in the property?"

"Well, some people from the county have proposed a trail there. It would connect to the Tobacco Heritage Trail, the Rails to Trails project. The old railroad trestle is gone, leaving no way to cross the river. The trail would need to course through the property to use the highway bridge to cross over."

"Oh, yeah. I did hear about that."

"It would cause no great impact on our reservation though. In fact, it could even be beneficial to us."

"I can see how it might." The Rails to Trails project creates hiking trails over the path of abandoned train tracks. It is funded largely by donations from tobacco companies. This environmentally friendly and government endorsed program would not be likely to use violence to promote itself. "Do you know of anyone who might kidnap a protester like this?"

"No. I only know of the groups we've discussed that would have a stake in this. One would not suspect them to be capable of foul play."

"Yeah. I wouldn't either. Oh, one more thing, Chief. I've studied Phillip Merit's cell phone, and I found this recording on it. Could you take a listen to this?"

"Okay."

Duffer laid the phone on the conference table. There were some rustling noises at first. Then, there were some rhythmic thumping sounds. *Pum-pum-pump ... pum-pum-pump.* It continued for about a minute. Chief Heathcock's face froze, as if he couldn't believe what he was hearing.

"What do you make of those sounds?" asked Duffer.

"Well...it sounds like drumbeats to me."

"That's what I thought too. Do you think it could be Native American?"

"I guess it could be. This is quite a mystery."

"And you aren't aware of any Native Americans who live in this area?"

"No. None that I know of."

Duffer was grasping at threads, trying to find some connection. "You still don't believe there are spirits there from an ancient Wyanoke burial ground, do you?"

"Who am I to say? Stranger things have happened." The chief looked dead serious. "In my experience, spirits work with the forces of nature—wind, rain, storms. Drums? Kidnapping? I have not heard of such things."

"Well, thanks for taking time to meet with me today. If you hear any talk about this, please let me know."

"Certainly, Detective. And good luck with your investigation."

Detective Duffer had watched Heathcock's reaction to the phone recording. He felt he had been truthful with his answers but still seemed to know more than he was letting on. Maybe this would at least have shaken the bushes and bring out some type of lead.

CHAPTER 16

The South Hill ER was clambering with its usual level of chaos. This Saturday Dr. Hardy was working the ten to ten "mid" shift. Nurse Patty came down the hall from the front triage area, escorting a young man who was limping.

"Gunshot wound! Room 8!" she announced. That was one of Dr. Hardy's assigned rooms. He raced over and met them in the exam area. There were blood drippings down the hallway.

"How did he come in?" he asked. All ambulances entered from the rear bay, not the triage area.

"A friend dropped him off," said Patty. "He's been shot in the left thigh."

"What happened?" he asked the patient.

"My friend had a 9 mm, and it accidentally fired." He was calm and composed. His left pant leg had a hole in the thigh, and the fabric around it was soaked with blood.

"Let's get your jeans off and sit up on the stretcher," said Patty. Dr. Hardy helped slide his jeans down, exposing his thighs and legs. There was a wound a third of the way down his thigh that was slowly trickling blood. Another smaller wound was on the left buttock. A purplish skin bruise traveled in a line between the holes in the skin.

"An entrance and exit wound," said Dr. Hardy. This appeared to be consistent with his story. "Any trouble walking?"

"No. Not really." This was a good indication that the bone

was not damaged. Dr. Hardy palpated along the tract between the puncture holes. There were no foreign bodies or hematomas. This kid was lucky. He checked the pulses and sensation and found no evidence of neurovascular damage.

"Okay. Let's get an x-ray and some antibiotics in you. I hope it's just a flesh wound," said the doctor.

"Me too," said the boy.

"He's a minor," said Patty. "His parents are on the way." When he started charting, Hardy saw that he was sixteen years old. It was thirty minutes before the x-rays were completed, and Dr. Hardy reviewed them on the Synapse viewer.

"Good. No bullet fragments or fractures," he thought aloud. He looked over at room 8 and noted a small crowd had gathered. Amongst them was Detective Bruce Duffer and Deputy Hudson. Hardy joined the group.

"I'm Dr. Hardy," he announced. "Are you Nathan's parents?"

"Yes!" answered the lady. The man nodded.

"He was lucky. The bullet traveled under the skin and out. There are no signs of any fragments or injury to the femur."

"Oh, thank God!" she said.

"I've prescribed an antibiotic, and he should have this checked by a surgeon in forty-eight hours."

"Of course. We'll do it. Thank you, Doctor."

Detective Duffer and Hudson had drifted out into the hallway. Duffer spoke as Hardy came out of the room.

"Dr. Hardy, I heard what you told Nathan's parents. I just want to confirm that the injuries were just as you described."

"Sure. Through and through trajectory without significant deep tissue injury."

"Right."

"We got some photos before they dressed it," said Hudson.

"Good. So, you think it's accidental? Like he describes?" asked Hardy.

"Seems like it. If you try to shoot someone, you usually aim for the abdomen, the chest, or the head. Hardly ever would you try to shoot someone in the ass!"

"Yeah. I see your point."

The detective's phone rang, and he stepped away to answer it. Hardy still could overhear part of the call. "What? You're not kidding?" He sounded excited. "Yeah. I'll be right there!" He hurried back to Deputy Hudson. "Hudson, can you check out the home of this shooting?"

"Yes, sir. Sure," said Hudson.

"Phillip Merit just showed up! I'm on the way out to his house now."

"Was that the tree sitter?" asked Hardy.

"Yep. Missing for five days. Gotta go."

"Sure. That's great!" said Hardy.

EMTs were pushing a stretcher in from the ambulance bay. They rolled past Detective Duffer as he headed out the ambulance entrance. There was a fireman on the litter with an oxygen mask on his face. An intense odor of smoke clung to him as he coughed forcefully. Duffer paused and looked back at the emergency crew as they passed by him. Hardy noticed that all of his excitement over finding the missing boy seemed to drain from his body. He appeared troubled as he turned away and walked slowly out through the sliding doors.

CHAPTER 17

Detective Duffer drove up to the home of Phillip Merit. It was in the Beechwood area along Lake Gaston. The house was a two-story building with plank siding above the stone that composed the lower third. The yard was populated with towering oaks, beech and pine trees. Duffer could easily see how this rural, lakefront residence would foster an appreciation of the environment.

Mrs. Merit met him at the door. "Detective Duffer, come on in." Her face was lit up, and her eyes were gleaming. "He's showering now and he'll be down in a few minutes. We can wait for him in the den." She led him into a spacious room with high ceilings. Large windows looked down over the lake behind the house. Almost instantly, they heard footsteps coming down the stairs.

"Phillip. Detective Duffer is here," Mrs. Merit said, looking out into the hall.

Phillip was drying his hair with a towel as he stepped into the den. He was wearing a T-shirt and sweatpants. His face had the makings of a beard. "Hi, Detective," he said.

"Phillip, we're so glad you're okay! You had us worried. Were you hurt in any way?"

"Naw. Just bumped my head when they were grabbing me from the tree house." He leaned forward so Duffer could see the small scab on his scalp. The detective felt a wave of relief knowing there hadn't been a scalping attempt.

"So, what can you tell me about your kidnappers?" He pulled out a hand-sized notepad.

"Well, there were two men, and they wore masks—kerchiefs over their faces like wild west bandits. And baseball-type caps."

"Good. Is there anything else you can describe about them?" Phillip appeared quite composed and rational about the ordeal. Duffer felt he could trust his descriptions.

"One was probably five-eight or nine, medium build. The other, close to six-foot and heavy-set. Oh, and the smaller one had a tattoo on his left forearm. It looked like an animal's head, maybe a bear."

"Okay. Great. How about their voices? Did they have any type of accents or distinctive features?"

"They didn't speak much. Mostly some mumbling and grunting. I couldn't detect any particular accents."

"Every detail is helpful. Did they tie you up or gag you?"

"No. But I was confined to one room."

"One room. What type of building was it?"

"It looked like an abandoned old farmhouse. I'm not sure if it was in North Carolina or Virginia. It was near the state line. I was locked in a single back room with a metal fencing panel covering the window."

"What did they feed you?" Mrs. Merit injected.

"Well, sandwiches, fried chicken, Hardees and McDonalds take out, and lukewarm coffee."

"Poor baby!" she added.

"So, tell me how you escaped," asked Duffer.

"Some of the wood was dry rotted, and I was able to work loose a couple of nails. Then I used them to unscrew one corner of the metal window cage."

"That was pretty resourceful," said Duffer.

"The guys were in and out at all times during the day but often left me alone there at night. I knew we were off in the woods somewhere. If I left at night, they would have trouble finding me in the dark."

"That was smart."

"When I made it to a road, I waited 'til daylight to try to stop a car. I didn't want to risk flagging down their pickup truck by mistake."

"Yeah. That was good thinking. Can you identify their truck?"

"I'm not sure. It was dark when they took me away. It is a gray-colored pickup, probably five to ten years old."

"Well, that's a start. Can you show me where you were picked up? Maybe we can start there and look for that farmhouse."

"Okay. When do you want to do this?"

"As soon as possible. Any leads out there are growing colder by the minute."

"All right. Just let me get dressed."

"Sure. I'll just wait outside until you're ready."

Detective Duffer sat out in his Crown Victoria, assimilating the information he had obtained. What could be the motive behind this abduction? It didn't fit the profile for human trafficking. Could this college kid, Phillip, be involved in drug dealing? The passenger door opening interrupted his train of thought.

"Okay, Detective. I'm ready," Phillip said, sliding into the passenger seat. "Just head down number one to road 903."

As they headed south, Phillip spoke again, with a bit of excitement. "So, how much ransom money did they ask for?"

Duffer paused briefly before speaking. He didn't want to make Phillip think he had been deemed worthless. "Son, we never received a ransom request."

"Oh." Phillip sounded downtrodden. "So...why was I abducted, then?"

"I don't know, Phillip." This was the honest truth. "It may have something to do with the dispute over the Mitchell Road property."

"So, I guess I was just a pawn, then."

"Likely so."

Phillip suddenly perked up. "Oh! It's just up here a ways."

They rode on a couple of minutes more before he pointed off to the right. "I got picked up near those pine trees!"

Duffer slowed down. "We're still on the Virginia side here."

"Yeah, but I walked for a couple of miles in the woods. Drive on a little further."

They crossed the North Carolina state line and, after a quarter of a mile, came to a dirt road. It led off the right side. "I think this is where they drove in," said Phillip.

The road was merely two parallel tire tracks entering the woods. Duffer noted that the tracks were fresh, appearing to have been made by a large truck. He glanced at his odometer to gauge how far down it might be to the site. Their progress was slow. After traveling 1.2 miles along the road, there appeared an open area.

"Oh, wow. It's been burned!" said Phillip.

"This was it?" asked Duffer.

There was a pile of blackened debris and a charred chimney still standing, overlooking the devastation. A few areas had gray smoke trickling upward from the ashes, filling the air with the pungent odor like a burning trash dump. The surrounding ground was marred with trampled wet mud and burnt brush.

"Yes. This was the house I was in."

It was obvious that this was no accident. An abandoned building, deep in the woods, burned to the ground—it reeked of arson. The kidnappers had sought to destroy all evidence of their crime. Phillip appeared devastated.

"There doesn't seem to be much left," said Duffer. "We'll sift through this debris once it's cooled down." He didn't reveal to Phillip that since this was in North Carolina and it was out of his jurisdiction.

CHAPTER 18

After dropping Phillip off, Detective Duffer drove back to his office. En route, he wasted no time in contacting the FBI field office in Richmond. He was told an agent would call him back in the next twenty-four hours. As he walked into his office, he scrolled through the contacts on his phone to the name "Nick." It was now four o'clock, or one o'clock on the West Coast. He had grown accustomed to Nick's daily reports. Nick had warned him that the fire involved areas that would take him out of cell phone range, possibly for days at a time. It had been three days since his last phone contact. Duffer pushed Nick's number on his phone. It rang repeatedly, ending with "The wireless customer you have reached has a mailbox that is full."

"Damn," thought Duffer aloud. His son was somewhere in the forty thousand acres of wildfires, on the other side of the continent, off the grid. He was battling a fire that had already claimed the lives of two firefighters. Seeing the fireman arriving in the ER earlier had driven home the reality of local responders being injured. Nick's risk was on a much grander scale.

The next morning was Sunday, and Duffer was at home. He was surprised to get a phone call from an unrecognized number. His hopes were high.

"Hello," he said hopefully.

"Detective Duffer?" The voice was not Nick's. His heart

sank. "This is FBI Agent Pruitt. I'm calling you back about an abduction."

"Oh? Yes. Agent Pruitt," said Duffer. "I'm surprised you called back on the weekend."

"Yeah. We take weekend duty too. So, what's the deal on this case down there?"

Detective Duffer recounted the kidnapping saga and the conflicts over the land acquisition. He told him of the captive house that was over the state border.

"So, no one claimed responsibility for the crime, and no ransom demand was ever received," said Agent Pruitt.

"That's right."

"This is a strange one."

"It seems that someone is trying to scare off buyers. First, the alleged Indian burial grounds and then the sudden disappearance of someone. Even the burning of the hostage house."

"Yeah. That sounds like a reasonable theory to me. We're sending a forensic unit down Monday to comb the burn site. I'll be at the sheriff's office then, too, and go over your files with you."

"Great. Thanks."

Detective Duffer was in his cubicle office Monday morning gathering together his notes. As promised, Agent Pruitt arrived at the sheriff's office around ten. Betsy brought the FBI agent to Duffer's office.

"Detective Duffer," she said. "Agent Pruitt from the FBI is here to see you."

"Thanks, Betsy." He extended his hand. "Agent Pruitt, I'm Bruce Duffer."

Agent Pruitt was of medium build, appearing to be in his mid-thirties. Instead of the traditional FBI dress shirt with black jacket and tie, he wore a golf-type shirt and khaki pants. He was clean cut and professional. They shook hands. He held a manila folder in his other hand.

"Good to meet you," said Pruitt. "I've started a file on the Phillip Merit abduction."

"Good. Betsy copied my notes for you." He handed the copies to Pruitt.

"The forensics unit is waiting outside. I guess we need to see the remains of the building and get started."

"Sure. Why don't you ride with me, and they can follow us there."

"That sounds good."

The black van followed Duffer and Pruitt to the scene. They drove down the wooded road to the house lot. It was cloudy, nearly overcast, but seemed appropriately gloomy. The burned structure was roped off with yellow crime scene tape. They got out and stood overlooking the site.

"If you'd like, I can drive you over to the abduction site in the woods," offered Duffer.

"Yeah. I'd like that," said Pruitt.

The crime scene team began working as they drove away toward Mitchell Road. When they arrived, they found a pickup truck parked near the "tree house."

"Wonder what this is," said Duffer as they parked. As they got out, two men in camouflage garb and blaze orange caps walked up from the woods. He suddenly remembered that bow hunting season had just begun. "Any luck, boys?" he asked.

"Yeah. But it was *bad* luck!" said the first hunter, who had a beard. He looked at Duffer's badge on the detective's belt. "Are you game wardens?"

"No. I'm Mecklenburg Detective Duffer, and this is Agent Pruitt." He noticed that they appeared a bit nervous. "Is there anything wrong?"

"Well, kind of," said the bearded hunter.

"We set up a couple of tree stands and a blind out here last week," the second hunter explained.

"We came out here this morning to hunt." The first hunter held up his crossbow.

"And we heard this chopping sound in the woods. Then, a loud cracking noise and found a tree fallen onto our deer blind!"

"It crushed it!"

"So, you're saying someone dropped a tree on your blind?" asked Detective Duffer.

"Yeah." They both nodded.

"Can you show us where this was?" he asked.

"Yeah, sure," said the second hunter. "It's back this way."

They walked about a hundred yards into the woods, dry leaves rustling about their feet, to reach the location. They found the camouflaged tent-like structure that was flattened by a fifteen- to eighteen-inch diameter tree that laid across it. If any occupants had been in the blind, this would most likely have been fatal.

"You can see why it scared us," said the hunter with the bow. "We were only about ten to fifteen yards away."

"About here," said the second hunter, stepping off to the side.

"Oh, my God!" said Duffer. "This is malicious endangerment. You could have been hurt or killed!"

He walked over to the base of the tree to examine the cutting. The tree had been chopped, the trunk was hammered with cut marks, and wood chunks were scattered on the ground. Lying amongst these fragments was a primitive tool. A triangular stone was mounted on a wooden handle. It looked like an over-sized tomahawk.

"Was it Indians?" asked the first hunter.

"I'm not sure." Duffer looked at Agent Pruitt. "But someone certainly wants us to think so."

"Did you see anyone around here?" asked Agent Pruitt.

"No," said the bearded man. "But I thought I saw an animal of some type running off. Like a coyote or maybe a bear."

Duffer thought that an animal would not be capable of this task. And a person would have frightened off any wild beasts. It just seemed odd.

"We'll see what we can find out about this," said Duffer.

CHAPTER 19

The summer had been unusually dry, even deemed a drought by the news weathermen. They were, however, prone to exaggerate the severity of the weather. Even in late October, it was still hot and arid near midday. Buck Warren had completed his dozer work on Dr. Hardy's pasture site. The terrain was now graded with a small spring pond on the side of the slope. It was also barren.

"You'll need some grass to keep it from washing," Buck had told Hardy. "'Bout the only thing that'll grow with it this hot and dry is millet."

"Okay. Thanks," said Hardy.

Dr. Hardy bought some millet seed. He thought it looked like bird feed. He poured some into the well of the spreader and mixed in some lime pellets and fertilizer. He pushed the plastic seeder back and forth along the dried clay. The clumps and dozer tread tracks made for a jerky job. He saw his wife driving along on the driveway beside the field. She was heading toward their house. He was feeling thirsty and realized that it was about lunchtime. "I'll go in after this load," he said to himself.

Lucy had gotten the mail, which was stacked on the kitchen island. Dr. Hardy leafed through it as he spoke.

"I thought I'd take a lunch break," he said.

"I was going to fix a tuna melt. Would you like one too?"

"Yeah. That'd be great."

He sat down and unfolded *The News Progress*, the weekly local paper he had selected from the postal pile. The front-page story caught his eye.

"Hey. They found that tree sitter who was missing."

"Was he dead?" asked Lucy.

"No. Apparently he was abducted."

"Why?"

"It doesn't say. Seems that it's a mystery. They mention the controversy over the property on Mitchell Road."

"So, no ransom, no human trafficking?" Lucy asked.

"I guess not."

Lucy placed the sandwiches on the bar top counter. "You would think they could find other properties in the state and not have to fight over that one."

"Well, with real estate, it's location, location, location."

"So, you think that sized tract on the lakefront is the reason?"

"Apparently so."

"Well, I wouldn't care if the Indians got it. At least it's not that beer brewery that was considering that site fifteen years ago," she said.

"Oh? So, if the Wyanoake tribe got it, you wouldn't have *reservations* about it?"

CHAPTER 20

FBI field agent Pruitt sat beside Detective Duffer's desk. He wore his blue polo-type shirt uniform. It had been a week since he began his investigation. Duffer was eager to hear his report.

"So, what have you got?" asked Duffer.

"Well, some enlightenment but no indict-en-ment, so to speak. Your ash house is on property owned by Dalton Timber Company. It was abandoned ten years ago."

"I'm not surprised." Duffer suddenly had a thought. *Could the timber company also be seeking the Mitchell Road property?* That could mean another suspect thrown into the lot.

"Well, here's the *enlightenment*. It was abandoned by the Silver family, descendants of the Weyanoke Indians."

"Oh?"

"They left it to move to the North Carolina reservation community."

"So, there's a link to the Native Americans." Duffer's interest had now been captured.

"But ... that's all the substance I can offer. Studying the ashes revealed only some metal household items and construction debris."

"But it was arson, wasn't it?"

"Oh, yes. We found evidence of accelerants in the forensics. Hydrocarbons, probably gasoline. I'll send you my written report in a few days. Again, no DNA, no fingerprints, no documents. Sorry."

"I didn't expect that you would find much," said Duffer, his hopes dampened. He paused before disclosing what else was on his mind. "A few months ago, some Indian relics were planted on the Mitchell property, trying to pass it off as an ancient tribal burial ground. Then, a tree sitter hears Indian drumbeats at night and later disappears mysteriously for days. And now, a tree was dropped on a hunting blind with, again, Indian relics found at the scene. Does this seem spooky to you?"

"Well, I might think twice before I'd set up my fragile solar panels out there, spirits or not."

"Yeah. Me too."

"Oh, we did find a couple of arrowheads," said Pruitt. He pulled a photo from the file. "See?"

"Projectile points," said Duffer.

"The technical production is authentic to Native Americans. But they're not old. Made in the last ten to twenty years."

"So, modern manufactured real projectile points." Somehow, the detective did not find this surprising. Just more Indian connections to this lakeside property.

Agent Pruitt stood up to leave. "Thanks for bringing us in on this case. I can't see where it may go from here, but we'll keep it on our radar. Keep up the fight for the right!"

"I'll try. Thanks again for your help. I can use all the input I can get."

Agent Pruitt had left Duffer with a few tidbits to chew on. He couldn't discount Chief Heathcock's involvement, but he always appeared clean when questioned. Plus, he was sincere and genuinely concerned for his people. Nonetheless, Duffer would have to meet with him again. Maybe on his turf this time.

Duffer's cell phone rang. He was a little irritated at the interruption. The caller's number was not familiar.

"Hello, Duffer here," he answered mechanically.

"Dad, it's Nick." A wave of relief flowed through Duffer's body.

"Nick! Are you okay, Son?"

"Yeah, Dad. I'm calling from a phone at our camp. Cell service here is spotty."

"I've been worried sick! Some firefighters have been killed."

"Yeah, I know. They were seventy miles south of us. It's been intense, but I feel like I've really helped out here. So much property has been destroyed."

"I know. They're lucky to have you there."

"What's new back home? I've been out of the loop here. We're pretty isolated."

"Not much new here. When do you come home?" Duffer felt that his son had certainly done his part already.

"Probably two to three weeks. I'll be glad to get home."

"You and me both, Son." He was certain he would be the one who was the happiest.

CHAPTER 21

The morning air was chilled, giving a sharp contrast to the profile of the countryside. Only a few wispy clouds interrupted the expansive deep blue sky. A light frost dusted the ground catching the rays from the low riding sun, sparkling like tiny sequins. The ponds and lake coves gave rise to smoke-like trails of fog as the water stubbornly held on to the warmth it had absorbed from the prior day. Detective Duffer was driving his Crown Vic, en route to meeting with Chief Heathcock. He had taken his unmarked car to be less conspicuous. His drive took him past the captive house entrance road. He looked briefly toward it as he passed. North Carolina was out of his jurisdiction, but this trip was not aimed at making any charges of crimes.

About twelve miles past Warrenton, he reached the community of Fishing Creek. There was a country store and another small brick building. A sign in front of the building read "Weyanoke Tribal Center." He parked in front and got out. Duffer was wearing a tan, golf-style shirt with a Mecklenburg County Sheriff's Department star embroidered on it. In his hand was a black nylon gym bag. He opened the door to find a woman seated at a computer desk.

"Hi, I'm Detective Duffer from Virginia," he said.

"Yes. We're expecting you," she said. Chief Heathcock emerged from the room behind her.

"Detective Duffer, come on back please," he said.

"Thank you, Chief Heathcock." They entered his office. It

was decent sized with photos of some executive-type people and powwow activities. Duffer's office cubicle paled in comparison. "Nice place you have here."

"Thank you. We do our business work here and have a conference room for meetings and social gatherings. What can I help you with today, Detective?"

"Well, I'm not sure. I've had some curious events happen, centered around the property you've been interested in back in Virginia."

"Oh?"

"Do you remember the protester tree sitter?"

"Yes, I do. It appeared he was unsuccessful in preventing the solar energy test site," said Heathcock.

"Yes . . . but we have verified that he was kidnapped too," said Duffer.

"Kidnapped? For what reason?"

"I'm not sure. No ransom was demanded. But he was held hostage in an abandoned house previously owned by one of your tribal members. A Mr. Silver."

"Oh. Do you think they were involved in this act?"

"I don't know, Chief. But this was found at the scene." The detective pulled the arrow out of the gym bag and handed it to Heathcock.

"Hmm," said Heathcock as he studied the stone arrowhead. "Turkey feather fletching. This is good work. I can see why you would think my people might be involved. It seems someone certainly wanted to implicate us."

"That's what I was thinking. An offender wouldn't likely leave evidence that might incriminate himself."

"Yes. I agree."

"But then, a week later, a tree was chopped down, falling on a hunting blind on that same property. And this was left at the scene." He pulled out the tomahawk and handed it to the chief.

"This is puzzling to me," said Heathcock.

"You can see my perspective. Do you know where these items might have come from?"

"No. But there is a tribal member here who makes projectile points. He sells them to tourists and at powwows. He might know more about this. I can take you to his home."

"That would be great," said Duffer.

Chief Heathcock drove them in his red Bronco. He said the body color represented the Native Americans. Duffer assumed it was from the term *redskins*, but Heathcock said, "The Native American name *Saponi* means red earth people."

They stopped in front of a small white house with an arrowhead-shaped sign at the edge of the yard. A man with a red headband came out to greet them. His dark, shoulder-length hair appeared tangled.

"George," said the chief. "This is Detective Duffer from Virginia."

"Hello," greeted George.

"He is interested in how projectile points are made."

"Yes, I am," said Duffer.

"Oh, good," said George, smiling. "Come out back to my shop." As they walked, he continued to speak. "First, the type of rock selection is most important. I like flint and quartzite, but there are a few good others." He led them into a small metal building behind his house. Inside, a long table stretched out along each side. One had various-sized stones on top and two stools beside it. The other had projectile points arranged by sizes. There were plastic storage boxes stacked under the table.

George picked up a stone larger than a fist and struck it with a hammer-like tool at an angle, flaking off some smaller fragments. He selected one of these to be shaped. His knapping tool looked like a wooden punch with a metal cap on one end. He used the tool to press down along the edges, chipping off tiny pieces.

"Early Native Americans often used bones or antlers as a tool for this flint knapping. You just keep chipping away at the edges until you get the desired shape."

"Wow," said Duffer, fascinated. "You mind if I video this?"

"No. Not at all."

"How long does it take you to make, say, an arrowhead?" Duffer aimed his cell phone at George's hand work.

"Sometimes as quick as twenty minutes, usually a bit longer."

"So, these projectile points on this table are the results of weeks of work."

"For sure," said George.

"Thanks for showing me this skill. It'll help me understand where my evidence came from."

"Evidence?" said George.

"Yeah. An arrow and a tomahawk. Do you want to see them?"

"Sure!"

Back at Heathcock's Bronco, Duffer opened the gym bag. George examined the arrow first.

"This is good work. Anyone who does flint knapping could have made this." He then studied the tomahawk. He stopped suddenly and pulled it in close. Looking up, he spoke in a serious tone. "I made this tool head!"

Duffer turned to Heathcock, then they both looked at George.

"Hey. I just chipped the stone. Someone else set it on this handle."

"Who?" asked Chief Heathcock.

"I wouldn't know. I just make these to sell. Anyone could have bought it at a powwow or a craft show."

"Someone who wanted to frame your tribe," said Duffer.

"Yeah. I guess," said George.

Back at the center, Heathcock and Duffer stood beside the red Bronco. Duffer offered his outstretched hand.

"Thanks, Chief. You've added another layer to the mystery," he said as they shook.

"I'm sorry if this is a bad reflection on my people. I trust you to seek the truth. For both of us."

"I'll do my best." He hoped his hopelessness was not obvious.

As he drove off, a tall slender man stepped out of the center. He had straight black hair in a ponytail and a tuft of hair under his lower lip. It looked like Hitler's mustache that had been inverted downward.

"Mr. Norton," said Heathcock. "Good to see you."

"Who's the cop?" asked the man.

"Oh, just a county officer from Virginia. Some stuff about the site we're seeking there."

"Good stuff, I hope."

"Well, I don't know for sure."

CHAPTER 22

Dr. Hardy found the ER shift from 10:00 AM to 10:00 PM to be the most draining. He often was too keyed up from work stress and caffeine to go directly to bed when he got home. It was usually around midnight when he got home and sometimes 2:00 AM before he climbed into bed. He was on the verge of waking up when his phone buzzed rudely.

"Dr. Hardy," he answered.

"This is Investigator Bennett from the ME's office. Are you available for a scene visit?"

"Maybe. Where is it?"

"It's in Bracey." That was on the way to the ER for Hardy. He glanced at the bedside clock–8:32 AM. It would give him forty to forty-five minutes time to work the scene.

"Yeah. I think so."

He got the directions from the investigator and quickly dressed for work in the ER. He grabbed his nylon ME bag, along with his ER sack that held his stethoscope, trail mix, and a soda. Lucy handed him a lunch bag and a travel mug of coffee as he bid her goodbye.

Hardy was familiar with the scene site as he knew of the property battle on Mitchell Road. He arrived at the location at 9:08, just as he swallowed his last mouthful of coffee. There was a small graveled parking lot that was new since he had last been by there. There was a van with the RAE logo on the side, an ambulance, a police cruiser, and a pale blue Crown Victoria. Bruce Duffer approached him as he got out of his Jeep.

"Good morning, Doc," he said.

"'Morning, Bruce. What ya got here?"

"Electrocution, apparently." They began walking toward a steel shed. A chain-link fence joined it on either side, flowing out in both directions to form the front boundary of a large square-shaped plot. The RAE logo was displayed prominently on the side. "He was out here to do a routine power monitor check on this solar field." There was an array of mirrored rectangular panels in parallel lines inside the fenced area, angled to face the sun.

"Is this operational?" asked Hardy.

"Well, yes. But it's just a test site for RAE."

"Oh, yeah?"

"He was wearing his insulated work gloves, but it looks like there was a power pulse flash."

Officer Hudson was standing in the entrance to the small metal building. Inside the doorway, half of the wall was covered by an electrical panel board. The far end was blackened and mangled. The body was lying out from the panel board.

"The decedent is Hank Jordan, a thirty-five-year-old male," he said. "He's an electrical technician for Radiant Acquired Energy. He was making a routine power check at 7:30 AM. He was supposed to call it in. His supervisor called him at 8:05, and again at 8:15, with no answer. He sent someone out to check on him, and this is what they found."

Mr. Jordan was positioned on his left side, facing up. He was a young adult Caucasian wearing light blue coveralls. He appeared to be about five eleven, 190 pounds. His work uniform was burned over the sleeves and ankle areas. There was a helmet lying on the floor above his head. The odor of burnt hair was oppressive. His facial skin was reddened with singed eyebrows and hairline. With blue gloves on, Dr. Hardy palpated the man's head and found no obvious fractures. Hardy rolled him onto his back, and a trickle of blood oozed out from his ear canal. *This could indicate a basilar skull fracture or ... a blast injury induced ear drum rupture*, thought Hardy. There appeared to be no other gross injuries.

He measured an axillary temperature using the meat thermometer from his ME bag—96.3°. This was consistent with a time of death occurring one to two hours prior.

"The time of death was probably 7:30 to 8:00 AM," said Hardy. "I think the explosion, the blast injury, was likely the cause of death. The Richmond office will do the postmortem to confirm the cause."

"Okay. Thanks, Doc," said Duffer.

Dr. Hardy drove off to work. *Eleven minutes 'til I'm due in the ER*. The CME-1 form would have to wait until he was off to complete. His mind was racing, trying to assimilate the death scene while rushing to work. He parked his Jeep at 10:01 and grabbed his ER bag. As he closed the driver's door, he realized the the bag he was holding was the ME bag. *This day's against me*, he thought, exchanging it for the bag in the passenger seat that contained his ER work items.

He power-walked to the ER, used his hospital ID card to open the ambulance bay doors, and positioned himself at a computer terminal. He logged in and claimed his first patient at 10:06.

Dr. Hardy promptly began examining the patient with a cough in room 8. Returning to his station, he entered the orders for a breathing treatment and a chest x-ray. The patient had said he was on "sleep-PAP" (CPAP) at night and used "nipple-lizer" (nebulizer) medications at home. He smiled and hoped he would remember to add these terms to his collection. Dr. Clint Taylor was at the terminal beside him.

"Did you oversleep, Hardy?" said Taylor.

"No. I had a *house call* to make on the way in."

"A house call? What's that about?"

"An ME case on a job site."

"Oh yeah? Sounds more interesting than what we have here."

"Yeah. It was. An occupational explosion. I guess he would have shown up *here* if he had survived."

"Okay. You're off the hook for being ten minutes late."

"Six minutes! But thanks. You know, so far today I've had a 50 percent patient mortality rate."

"Wow! You're improving!" said Taylor, smiling at his coworker.

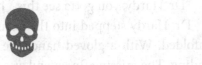

CHAPTER 23

"**F**inger injury, room 9," called out the triage nurse. She pushed a man in a wheelchair by and delivered him to the announced room. A male nurse joined them and began preparing the patient for treatment. Dr. Hardy came over to the exam room.

"I'm Dr. Hardy. What's happened to you?"

The man was wearing a flannel shirt and jeans. He had bloody gauze wrapped over the end of his right index finger.

"I was climbing down from my tree stand and the step collapsed. I grabbed the metal seat and tore off my finger!" He pulled off the dressing and revealed that the distal finger was missing. Some blood was oozing from the nub.

"My God!" said Hardy. He quickly composed from his surprise and stated matter-of-factly, "Did you find the missing end?"

"No. I looked around briefly, but then just rushed on in."

"Okay. No problem." Hardy realized that finger reattachment was a delicate, specialized procedure. He would administer antibiotics and refer him to the hand surgeon in Richmond, with or without the severed part. "We'll x-ray your hand to determine the bone and joint damage and then transfer you to MCV."

"Okay. Do what you can."

The x-ray was done in the exam room. As the doctor was viewing the images on the portable machine, another man and a woman ran excitedly into the room. They were carefully carrying a towel. The male nurse came over to Hardy.

"Dr. Hardy, you gotta see this," he said.

Dr. Hardy stepped into the exam room where the towel was unfolded. With a gloved hand, the nurse picked up the prized finding. The missing finger end was there with a long, one foot in length, string dangling out from it.

"We had been looking all over the ground," said the male visitor.

"Then, I looked up and this was dangling from the tree stand," said the woman.

Dr. Hardy looked closer. The "string" was a fibrous white, glistening structure. He realized that this was the tendon that had been ripped out of his forearm! He turned to the nurse.

"Rinse this off good in saline, wrap it in gauze, and ice it down. They'll be headed to Richmond."

After the excitement of the string-finger man being transferred to MCV, Dr. Hardy completed a more mundane ER shift. He started home at 10:55 PM. As he left the parking lot, he called Lucy on his cell phone.

"I'm leaving South Hill now. I still have a ME case to complete tonight."

"Okay. See you soon. Do you want a snack when you get here?"

"Maybe. Thanks. Love you."

"Love you too."

As soon as he got home, he spread his notes on the bar top in the kitchen. Lucy handed him a slice of reheated cheese pizza. He knew the autopsy would be done in the morning and they would want his scene report to review. He drew out the scene diagram and wrote up the demographics and description. Almost as a celebration, he grabbed a mini bottle of Cabernet Sauvignon from the four-pack carton and poured it into a glass.

"Lucy, can you scan this into the fax?" he asked.

"Sure." She took the pages to her scanner.

"Oh, I got a couple of new words from a patient today."

"Yeah? When are you ever gonna publish this book?"

"Well, I need to draw up some cartoon illustrations, you know."

"Sure. Just do it in your *spare time*," she said jokingly.

"Yeah, I know. Oh, I had a hunting accident come in today."

"A gunshot wound?"

"No. A fingertip amputation. A man fell from a tree stand and tore off his finger with a long tendon hanging off it."

"Gross!"

"Yeah. An unrecognized, rare danger of hunting."

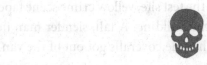

CHAPTER 24

Duffer's secretary's voice came through on his speaker phone.

"Bruce. Realtor Bill Bradson is on line one."

"Thanks," said Duffer, punching line one. "Detective Duffer here."

"Bruce, it's Bill Bradson. I just got an unusual call and thought I'd give you a head's up."

"Oh, yeah? What's up?"

"Logan Dalton, from Dalton Timber Company, called me. He asked about the availability of the Thompson's estate on Mitchell Road. He thinks the solar company may want to abandon their option after an accident they had there."

"Oh? That is interesting." Details of the tragedy there had not been released yet.

"Yeah. I heard y'all were investigating an incident, and it's odd he asked about this now. I told him I'd get back to him."

"Thanks. It is odd, indeed. Thanks for the tip, Bill."

"Sure. Anytime."

Duffer had felt the "accident" at the test site was suspicious. This only reinforced his instincts. He was a fire investigator for the sheriff's department and had worked the scene, taking photos and collecting samples. He checked his watch. A RAE electrician was scheduled to meet him at the scene at 9:30 AM.

"I'll be out on Mitchell Road," he said to Betsy as he left the office.

A RAE van was parked at the test site, yellow crime scene tape still crossed the doorway of the building. A tall, slender man in black-rimmed glasses and light-blue coveralls got out of the van. Duffer walked up to him.

"I'm Bruce Duffer."

"Randy Arnold, with Radiant Acquired Energy," said the man.

"There is evidence of a fire and an explosion here," said Duffer, ducking under the tape to lead them through the doorway. "I've sent samples for accelerant testing and chemical composition."

Randy studied the distorted panel and proceeded to look behind it. Solid, vertical box-like structures stood there, about two feet tall. Many of those nearest to the wall panels were split and mangled.

"These are lead acid batteries, similar to automobile batteries," he stated. "They are cheap but functional. That's why they were employed at this test site."

"Do you think they were the source of the blast?"

"Yep. I'm certain. As they charge, hydrogen gas accumulates. It's normally contained in the casing. If there is a crack or break, it will be released. Some of these batteries are showing holes drilled in the casings." He pointed to several of the largely intact batteries. "Hydrogen gas, by itself, is not that dangerous. But a spark can ignite it."

Like the Hindenburg, thought Duffer.

The back of the distorted panel still displayed some intact wiring. Randy scrutinized the array a moment before commenting.

"The ground wire is not connected to ground. I think it was moved deliberately. If it was near a battery terminal, it would spark when the master switch was thrown. That's what Hank came out here to do, to test the voltage level."

"So, his insulated gloves protected him from electrical current but a spark exploded the hydrogen gas, like a propane explosion in someone's home."

"Yeah. It's pretty clear to me."

"I see." He paused pensively. "That makes this murder, first degree. Randy, I'll need you to prepare a written report of your findings."

"Sure. I was planning to anyway. This is sabotage against RAE."

"That's true. I'll send you the fire forensics report as soon as it's complete. How can I get a list of people who had access to this test site?"

"I'll request it for you. You may need a warrant for it."

"No problem. I'll get it. Thanks for your expertise."

"Sure thing."

Duffer headed back to his office. This killing obviously took some plotting and engineering to orchestrate. The Mecklenburg Forest Preservation group did not seem capable of such violence. They were inadequately organized and had no corporate backing for it. His suspects now seemed to include Dalton Timber Company and the Weyanoke Tribe.

I need to talk to Logan Dalton, he thought. When he reached Route 1, instead of turning right toward his office, he turned left, heading away. Dalton Timber Company was in Palmer Springs, and an impromptu visit might provide some clues.

The lumber company's base office site had two large steel shed-like buildings. They were tan and had gray roofs with gravel between them. The sides were open and housed bulldozers, hydraulic tree harvesters, and cranes. An eighteen-wheeled log truck was parked alongside one structure. A third building sat back, at a right angle to the sheds and was warehouse style. On the right corner of this building was a door with a sign over it reading "Office." Duffer parked near this door and entered.

There was a window inside to the right. On the front wall were mounted five plaques of cross-sectioned trees labeled as five, ten, fifteen, twenty, and twenty-five years. On the back wall was a poster. It was a parody of the evolution of man that pictured an ape, primitive man forms, and modern man on the far right. This, however, depicted a primitive man holding a tomahawk, the next figure an ax, followed by an old hand crosscut saw, and a modern man with a chainsaw. A middle-aged appearing woman sat at a metal desk.

"Can we help you?" she asked. Behind her stood a slightly heavy-set man with black hair and beard. He was holding what appeared to be bills or invoices.

"Yes. I'm Detective Duffer. I was wondering if I could speak with someone regarding the Mitchell Road property."

"Oh, yeah?" said the man. "I'm Logan Dalton. I know that property. What about it?"

"Bill Bradson says you recently called him inquiring about that property."

"Yeah. It would be a good timber tract for my company. We currently manage about fourteen hundred acres in two states. We'd love to buy it. It would be a shame to waste it by covering it with a bunch of solar panels."

"I reckon so. But you know they have an option on it and have set up a test site there."

"Yeah, I know. But I heard they've had some problems with it." His voice was steady, no evidence of anxiety or stress.

"Oh? What did you hear?" Most of the details were not public yet.

"Just that there was some big accident out there yesterday."

"Oh, yeah? Tell me just how you heard about it?" Duffer was probing but trying not to be accusatory.

"One of my employees said something."

"How did they hear about it?"

"I think they said their friend was on the rescue squad crew that responded. Why? Was this more than just an accident?"

"We're investigating it now." Logan didn't seem to know that there was a fatality. Maybe his interest was merely opportunistic. "There was a fire on some of your property in Warren County about six weeks ago, wasn't it?"

"Yeah. The abandoned farmhouse." He shook his head.

"Damn. We lost five acres of timber with that. There was an FBI agent who came by asking me about that too."

"Probably Agent Pruitt."

"Yes! That's right."

Duffer had sensed nothing suspicious from Dalton so far. "Well, thanks for speaking with me today."

"No problem. Hey, if that land does become available, I'm still interested in it."

"Sure. Noted." As he turned to leave, he looked back at Dalton. "Oh, by the way, have you noticed any unusual Native American activities on any of your properties?"

"No, not since they found that skull out on Mitchell Road."

"Okay. Thanks for your help." He didn't feel it was necessary to ask for a list of employees. Nothing here seemed the least bit out of order. When he complained about losing "five acres" in the fire, he couldn't help but think of Nick out in forty thousand acres of wildfires in California.

"God, I'd like see him now," he thought aloud.

CHAPTER 25

It was Wednesday morning, and Dr. Hardy was off of work. He sat at the kitchen bar of his home where papers were spread about. He had started working on his book of laymen's medical misnomers that he had been collecting. Most of the papers were scraps that had rough sketches of cartoons on them. In the center of the array was a large sketch pad where he was carefully drafting his animations. Black ink figures "spoke" in diagrammed bubbles. A figure of a man was depicted saying, "The doctor says I have infection in my **limp** glands and **described** me some **erector-mycin**." He was hoping to create fifteen to twenty drawings.

Lucy came in with the morning mail. "That mail girl is slow. She should come by before eleven and now it's almost noon," she said.

"Anything interesting?" asked Hardy.

"No. Just sales fliers and the newspaper."

"Oh." He took the newspaper and began skimming over it. He welcomed a break from his drawing. One article caught his attention: "Solar Power Worker Murdered at Test Site," he read. "Did you see this?"

"What?" said Lucy.

"That man killed in the explosion out on Mitchell Road was murdered. It appears the site was sabotaged, and the blast was rigged."

"That's awful!"

"It could be the Mecklenburg Forest Preservation group or, possibly, the electric co-op, if solar power presents a threat to them. I wonder if RAE will abandon its plans for the solar farm now. It seems like it's not worth all the fight."

"Personally, I think the Indians should get it."

Dr. Hardy thought that the Weyanoke tribe might be murder suspects as well. "Oh, that's right. You're part Indian too. How much Indian?"

"At least one-eighth."

"So ... could you set up some land as a *reservation*?"

"No. But I could potentially join a tribe. For a reservation, you have to have several generations of designated Native Americans inhabiting a community. Then, they can file with the government for establishment."

"I see. Nothing's that easy, huh?"

"Yeah. Do you know why they call Native Americans the Indian Nation?"

"I guess because the tribes are somewhat similar groups."

"Well, yes, but the reservations form a separate territory *nation*. They are not subject to US laws or governance. They are all independent of governing, taxes, policing, courts, and jails."

"That takes a lot of organization and public expenses."

"Yes. Some smaller reservations contract with county police and court systems to help manage their community."

"Oh, now that would be advantageous for both."

"Yeah."

Bruce Duffer had Native Americans on his mind as well. He had driven to Lawrenceville, to the Fort Christanna site. The fort was one of two that were established in Virginia in 1715 by Governor Spotswood. It served to protect the indigenous population from rebellious American colonists as well as other hostile tribes. The detective paused to read the historic marker plaque. The brief statement only hinted at the role this site played in the tangled saga of Native American people of this region. This fort had been populated by about three hundred Native Americans, predominantly the Saponi Confederation. The Saponi had allied with the Catawba Confederation as they shared cultural traits and similar linguistics. Duffer felt certain that some members of the Weyanoke had sought refuge here as well. He smiled as he looked at the design of the fort. It had been shaped in a pentagon layout, a design the United States copied outside of Washington, DC.

Just south of this fort, in North Carolina, the Haliwarnash Croatan Indian Club formed in the 1940s. Their name was a composite of the names of Halifax, Warren, and Nash counties. Tribal members banded together from Saponi, Tuscarom, Occoneechee, Tutelo, and Nansemond origins. Many of the Saponi had migrated south to escape aggressive advances of the Iroquois in New York and Pennsylvania. As the membership shifted, the name was shortened to just Haliwa Indian Club. Its membership now totaled over four thousand. The Weyanoke had only a few hundred surviving members.

Duffer wandered about the field where the booths were set up; drumbeats and flute-like music filled the air. It was a mild day for early November, about sixty-eight degrees and sunny. There was an occasional mild breeze, but the small clouds in the sky stood motionless. Many tribal members were dressed in celebratory Native American garb or regalia. They were adorned in feathered headdresses and colorful vests with necklaces of leather pendants.

He had no specific agenda for his attendance, only a slim hope that some clue might arise. Since he was "off duty," he wasn't wearing his badge or sheriff's department shirt. He bought a corn dog and ambled about while he ate it. One table was selling Native American jewelry, another displayed woven net dream catchers adorned with various beads and feathers. One booth in particular caught his full attention. It had a spread of arrowheads and tomahawks. Not the cheap plastic toys that some others were selling to kids, but real stone-worked points. Behind the tables, complete arrows, spears, and tomahawks were mounted. He drew near and studied the molded stones, remembering the knapping process George had demonstrated.

As he picked up a projectile point for closer inspection, the attendant said, "See anything you like?"

"Just admiring the work," he answered. "These are pretty neat."

"Yeah. Genuine, handmade by Native Americans." The man appeared to be in his thirties, short-statured with black hair and tanned skin. "I like these," he said, picking up a point that was made of quartz. Duffer noted a tattoo on the man's left forearm. The ink was an animal head, probably a bear. Something clicked in the detective's mind.

Where have I heard of a bear's head tattoo? he thought. "Yeah. It's a beauty. Can you hold it up and let me get a picture of it?"

"Sure."

Duffer used his cell phone to take two photos, making sure he included the left forearm in the shots. "Thanks. That's some good work. I may be back by. Do you have a card?"

"No, I don't."

"Okay."

As he turned to walk away, he suddenly thought, *Phillip Merit!*. He had described one of the kidnappers with an animal head tattoo. *I need some more face and body photos,* he thought. He took a few steps away and turned back toward the booth. Pretending to be photographing the whole powwow array, he panned back to the salesman, getting some extra views. Maybe this would be something to go on.

Detective Duffer felt a little excited. He decided to drive directly to the Merit home on his trip back home. Luckily, Phillip Merit was at home when Duffer arrived. He showed him the pics on his phone.

"Well, I told you they were masked whenever I saw them.

But, yeah. He seems like the right size, and that appears to be the tattoo," said Phillip. "That could be him."

"That's the best I could expect from you, given the circumstances," said Duffer. "We'll see if this goes anywhere." Finally, a bit of a clue in this case.

First thing Monday morning, Detective Duffer moved his phone photos to a computer file. He printed the best shots for his office file. All of them were sent electronically to FBI Agent Pruitt. He included the message: "This man is a suspect in the kidnapping case. The victim identified the tattoos. He sells arrowheads at Indian powwows."

CHAPTER 26

"**B**ruce," said Betsy. "The FBI is on line 1."

"Okay, thanks." It was Wednesday morning, and Detective Duffer was at his work desk. He picked up the phone. "Detective Duffer here."

"Detective, this is Agent Pruitt. I was calling you back about the man in the pictures you sent me."

"Oh, yeah. I showed the pictures to Phillip Merit, the kidnapping victim. He thinks that it's the same one he saw on one of the kidnappers."

"Yeah. Good investigative work. We ran facial recognition screenings and questioned the powwow organizers. We've IDed the man as Jay Zimmer."

"Jay Zimmer. Thanks. I can run a record search."

"Already done. He had a breaking and entering charge in North Carolina in 2018 and a couple of DUIs. Not clean, but not a major criminal."

"What does he do?"

"He hangs out with Indian tribes, no stable address. Odd jobs. His most recent employment was for a solar power company."

"Was the company RAE?" asked Duffer.

"Ah, yes, I believe that's the one."

"There was a murder at the RAE test site last week. The battery units were tampered with to cause an explosion."

"When was this?"

113

"Thursday. I've requested a list of RAE employees who had access to the site."

"Okay. Good. Let me know if his name's on that list."

"Will do."

"Thanks for the intel. We won't move in on him until we have more evidence, but he looks hot."

"I guess at least we have something to work with."

"Yes. Good work, Bruce. We'll be back in touch."

"Okay. Thanks." He hung up the phone.

Jay Zimmer. A possible kidnapper, he thought. *And he works for RAE!* He had already subpoenaed the employee list but hadn't heard back. "Betsy," he said into the intercom. "Can you call RAE and see if they have our list of employees that had access to the test site ready yet?"

"Sure, Bruce."

Within thirty minutes, he received an email from RAE with the roster. Only eight names were on the list, one was Hank Jordan, the decedent. And Jay Zimmer was on the list!

"Betsy. Get Agent Pruitt back on the line," he asked.

"Okay."

RAE's local office was in Henderson, North Carolina, out of his jurisdiction. He needed the help of the FBI.

"Line 1, Bruce," came Betsy's voice.

"Thanks." He punched the speaker phone. "Agent Pruitt?"

"Yes, Detective."

"I got the list of RAE employees who had access to the test site. Jay Zimmer was one of them."

"Bingo! If you cross paths with him, do NOT arrest him. We will monitor him first. There must be an accomplice, and the motive is still vague. I'll let you know when we have enough to move in on."

"Okay. I guess he's just a POI for now?"

"Exactly. Thanks for the update."

So, a kidnapping and murder suspect but Duffer could only sit on his hands for now. This was frustrating.

The following day was court day, and Duffer had to be present for a criminal case he had worked, a breaking-and-entering case. Domestic and civil cases were heard in the same building as the sheriff's office. This case, however, was at the county courthouse in the center of town. The court was in a large white building with tall columns on the front porch. This county building's distinctive architectural feature was it had six columns instead of the standard four. Duffer was known to the officer manning the weapons screening, and he was waved past the metal detector. He walked by, file folder in hand, carrying his cell phone and 9mm Glock.

In the front hallway, he saw Dr. Hardy. "What brings you to court today?" he asked. They walked briefly together toward the stairway.

"Well, I treated an assault victim in the ER. I have to testify on the extent of the injuries."

"Okay. Not a fatality like your ME investigations, I hope."

"Oh, no," laughed Hardy. "Hey, I just saw Bill Bradson down the hall. He's been trying to sell my old house. He said he was on the way to the zoning office. Something about working an angle on the property out on Mitchell Road. I know you're investigating that murder we saw out there. Just an FYI."

"Yeah. Thanks." *A kidnapping there, too,* he thought. "I'll follow up with him on that."

"Sure. See you later." Dr. Hardy walked off to his appointed courtroom.

Detective Duffer opened one of the double doors to the rear of the general district courtroom. He found a seat near the rear of the room. Here he would await his turn on the court docket.

Bill Bradson, he thought. *What would he be doing in the zoning office?* Maybe he would visit the realtor's office after his court case.

CHAPTER 27

Detective Duffer walked out of the courthouse, relieved that his case was decided as a conviction. It was good to see the sky and feel the November air. The temperature was a mild sixty-two degrees. Bill Bradson's realtor office was on the next block. The county courthouse was truly the hub of the small town. Lining the four streets of the courthouse block were the library, bank, lawyer's office, restaurant, town hall, and pharmacy. He walked across the street to the realtor's office.

"Is Bill in?" he asked the secretary.

"Sure, Mr. Duffer. You can go right in," she said, nodding toward his office.

"Bruce Duffer," said Bradson. "Come on in. What can I help you with?"

Duffer pulled the door closed. "Well, nothing major. I was just curious about your interest in the zoning designation of the parcel on Mitchell Road. I've been doing some investigating about some incidents out there."

"Well, I'm sure you know about the controversy surrounding the potential sale of the property."

"Do I ever."

"So, I'm trying to orchestrate an outcome that mutually benefits all parties."

"That would be a miracle." This was a curious development, indeed. "What are you proposing?"

"The tract is three hundred acres, right? The logging company wants it for farming timber. The solar company wants it for a solar farm. But, they would be just as happy with a long-term lease. The Indians want a designated territory for establishing a future reservation. So, say the Native Americans buy two hundred acres and Dalton Timber Company the other one hundred acres. Dalton clean cuts one hundred acres of the Native American property for the RAE solar power farm, and they sign a twenty-year lease with the Indians. Also, the Native Americans plan to clear about sixty acres initially. Dalton would cut this tract as well, sharing the profit with the Native Americans. This way, they need less money to buy only two hundred acres versus three hundred. Plus, they get RAE lease revenue and a kickback from the logging profits as well. Dalton Timber Company still has one hundred acres to farm trees on. It seems like a win-win-win proposal!"

"Hey, that sounds good to me too," said Duffer. He really did admire this plan.

"I'll just need to get the county's approval for the appropriate zoning. Currently, it's all zoned agricultural. That's fine for tree farming. RAE needs commercial or, probably, industrial zoning. The Native Americans need residential with some business zoning."

"What do you have to do to change the zoning?"

"I just filed a request, and the county board of supervisors will review it. If they can't decide, it would go before the judge or, at worst, be sent out as a referendum to be voted on."

"I see. I hope this can work out for all parties."

"Yeah. Me too."

It was two weeks before the next county board of supervisors meeting. Duffer's wife, Ann, served on the board, and he accompanied her to the meeting in the town hall. Evelyn Merit, from the Mecklenburg Forest Preservation, was the chairman and introduced Bill Bradson. He presented his proposal for the usage of the Mitchell Road property to the board. Mrs. Merit then summarized his request.

"So, you propose making one hundred acres industrial, or possibly commercial, for solar panels. And one hundred acres residential with some business."

"Yes, but the Dalton Timber acreage would remain agricultural, for the present time," said Bradson.

"I feel that Native Americans respect the earth and live in harmony with their environment. This goes far for forest preservation in Mecklenburg County. I have no problems allowing the residential and business zoning under these circumstances," said Mrs. Merit.

"I agree," said a male board member. "The industrial-commercial designation for the other one hundred acres that will produce environmentally friendly energy also seems acceptable. After all, the Weyanoke will retain ownership throughout the solar lease."

"I might add," said Ann, "they already have had court approval for the one-acre test site."

The others voiced comments on the proposal and the vote subsequently was for approval. Bradson left the meeting smiling. Duffer felt a sense of satisfaction but, more so, of relief that the skirmishing over the now tainted territory might come to an end.

"Chief Heathcock should be happy," he said to his wife as they left.

His phone rang as he drove home with his wife. When he saw their son's number on the screen, he felt a warm surge through his body.

"Hello, Nick?" he answered. Ann suddenly looked his way. He changed his phone to speaker.

"Yeah. Hi, Dad." The familiar voice of his son soothed him.

"I'm here, too!" Ann interjected.

"Wow. I've missed you and Virginia."

"How are you, Son? What's happening there?" said Duffer.

"I'm good. A little tired. How are you?"

"We're fine," said Duffer.

"We've missed you, too," said Ann. "When are you coming home?" She sounded eager.

"Well, I'm planning for next week. I've already bought a ticket."

"Next week? That's Thanksgiving! That's great!" said Ann.

"I can't wait to see you, Son."

"Yeah. I can't wait to get home. We've done some good work out here, but the devastation has been enormous. So many homes have been destroyed. Such a waste."

"You've done good, Son. I love you," said Duffer.

"Yes. I love you, too," said Ann. "And I'm very proud of my little boy!"

"Thanks. I love y'all, too!"

CHAPTER 28

It was Monday afternoon when Detective Duffer was at the South Hill ER. He was dispatched to investigate an overdose victim. The subject was a twenty-two-year-old white female. "Friends" had found her unresponsive, and Deputy Hudson was the first on the scene. At the residence, he administered intranasal naloxone (Narcan) and she slowly awakened.

"Did you find any needle tracts?" Duffer asked Dr. Hardy, the on-duty ER physician.

"Yeah," said Hardy. "Mostly on the left forearm. I think she is right-handed."

"Okay. Anything else in her system?"

"Well, yes. Alcohol level 118 and urine drug screen was positive for opiates, marijuana, and cocaine."

"Okay. Thanks." He shook his head. "A walking medicine cabinet."

"You got it," said the doctor.

The detective went in to question the patient. His inquiries got the usual "I don't know" and "I can't remember" responses. He came out of the room and found Dr. Hardy at the doctors' work station.

"Pretty useless interrogation," he said.

"Yeah. I figured as much," said Hardy. "Hey, I read in the paper that they were rezoning the property on Mitchell Road. What's up with that?"

"Well, it's Bill Bradson's brainstorm. So far, it's looking to be a good resolution."

"Good. That's all right, then."

Duffer's cell phone rang. "Okay, Doc, I'll see you later," he said, walking off. "Duffer here."

"Hey, Bruce. Pruitt here."

"Good to hear from you. Any good news?"

"I'm afraid not. Zimmer never returned to work for RAE after the murder. And he has no known address."

"Oh. Sorry to hear that." It seemed like one step forward and two steps backward.

"It seems he drifts around but prefers the Native American territories. However, he is not registered as any tribal member."

"So, where do we go from here?"

"We'll start snooping around the Indian territories looking for leads. I'm going to start calling you every Monday to give regular updates. That way, we can keep working this from all angles."

"That's good. I appreciate that as well as today's update."

"No problem. I'll be talking to you next week."

"Okay. Thanks."

Duffer felt despair, now that his prime suspect had disappeared. He apparently lives off the grid. *Maybe Chief Heathcock would have some insight,* he thought. *Crap!* Pruitt had asked him to stay clear of Zimmer. He felt himself useless in this investigation.

He returned to the office to file his report on the overdose. He had not found anyone to file charges against. This was typical, even in cases with fatalities. Nobody knows nothing about nothing. He finished up and left work. He figured he might be home early enough for supper. Turning down Camp Bibee Drive, he drove on, turning into his driveway.

As he came in the front door, Ann was standing in the hall. Her brown hair with strands of gray was falling down onto her shoulders. She was grinning like the cat that swallowed the canary.

"I've got a surprise for you," she said.

"Oh, yeah?" said Bruce.

"I'm home!" said Nick, stepping out from the living room.

"Nick!" He rushed to hug his son.

"It's an early Thanksgiving," said Nick. Usually clean cut, he had shaggy hair growth and a beard. Nonetheless, Bruce thought that he never looked better.

"I picked him up at the airport this afternoon," said Ann. She was beaming. Bruce was so overjoyed that his eyes were filled with water.

"We were so worried about you, Son," he said. "But that was a great thing you did."

"I guess. But California lost 281,800 acres and 1,063 structures."

"Well, you know that your help prevented the loss of even more forest and homes," said Duffer.

"Well, I hope so, anyway."

They ate together for the first time in over two months. The homecoming dinner was Ann's fried chicken, mashed potatoes, and green beans. Catching up on the local news and stories of the forest fire dominated the mealtime conversation. After they finished eating and were clearing the table, Nick stepped out of the kitchen, saying, "I've got something I want to show you."

He returned and placed a cardboard box on the kitchen table. "The wildfire temperatures are usually about 800 degrees. Sometimes, when conditions are right, it can reach 1,400 to 1,600 degrees. When that happens ..." He opened the box. "You can find these!"

The box was full of shiny but irregularly shaped objects separated by newspaper. They were rounded, many multilobular, in various sizes. Nick picked out several and laid them on a placemat.

"What are these?" asked Ann curiously.

"Molten glass, mostly from windows of burned structures."

"They're great," said Duffer.

"Yeah. I thought it was neat."

"So, these are souvenirs of the disaster?" asked Ann.

"Well, sort of. I'm gonna put some in the rock tumbler and see how well they polish up. Maybe I could even sell some as, you know, *wildfire gems* or *fire drops*. I could give some of the money to support firefighters."

"Hey. I know a burn site you could search over to find some more of these," said Duffer. He thought of the burned kidnapping house and wondered if it had any glass windows that melted. "I'll check with Dalton Timber to see if it's okay to treasure hunt there."

"Great! Thanks, Dad."

CHAPTER 29

The next morning, Detective Duffer scraped a thin frosting of ice off the windshield of his Crown Victoria before leaving the house. He and Nick then drove out to Dalton Timber Company. By the time they reached the logging office, the light frost on the ground had melted. The cool morning air still gave rise to a smoky vapor forming from their exhaled breaths. They found Logan Dalton in his company's office.

"Detective Duffer," he said. "What brings you out here this morning?"

"Mr. Dalton, this is my son, Nick," said Duffer. "We have a favor to ask of you."

"Okay. Nice to meet you, Nick. What can I do for you?"

"Nick is a firefighter and he just got back from helping fight the California wildfires."

"Oh, yeah? I've seen that on the news."

"Well, Nick salvaged some molten glass nuggets from some of the burnt buildings. I wondered if there might be some fragments at the site where that abandoned house burned down on your property. And if you might permit him to salvage any from there."

"Hmm. That sounds interesting. Sure. It's nothing but ashes to me."

"Thanks. That's great," said Nick.

"We certainly appreciate this," said Duffer. "Hey, how's the project on Mitchell Road going for you?"

"Great, so far. We've started logging out on the Weyanoke section. We cut a road in there and have begun clearing some acres. Some good logs. Not bad for unplanted wild growth. Volunteer timber. The big harvest will be on the solar farm site. Wood prices are pretty good right now. Hardwoods bring about $150 per log."

"Good. We might drive by there on the way home."

"Sure. Have a look and see."

"Okay. And thanks again," said Duffer.

He drove out to the burned building with Nick. As they maneuvered the rutted road, Nick seemed to be studying the trees in admiration, so contrasted from the scorched acres he had seen. When they reached the scathed house site, Nick put on some blue gloves and began picking through the ashes.

"This fire wasn't hot enough," he concluded. "The few glass fragments here are not melted."

"I was afraid of that," said Duffer. It was just a single-story, old dried-wood building."

"Well, no harm in looking."

As they were reentering Virginia, Duffer's curiosity over the Mitchell Property had him headed down that road. There was a fairly wide dirt and gravel road cut down through the parcel near the center. He turned onto the road to have a look at the property.

"This is the site that was fought over by the solar power company, the conservationists, the timber company, and the Native Americans," Duffer explained to Nick. "They finally reached a compromise that's somewhat beneficial to all."

At the end of the road, they found some people standing around. Among them, Duffer recognized Chief Heathcock. Duffer got out of his car and approached him. A tall slender man stood just back behind Heathcock. He appeared less noble.

"Chief. Looks like it's finally happening," said Duffer, smiling.

"Yes, Detective. We are happy with the arrangements so far."

"Good. Oh, and this is my son, Nick."

They exchanged greetings.

"I am pleased that the Weyanoke will have a place of their own. And at such a splendid location," said the chief. "This is actually just a few miles down river from the original Occoneechee territories."

"Yeah. I'm glad for you."

As he gazed out toward the river, the chief's smile turned somber. "Your Agent Pruitt was inquiring about an associate. Jay Zimmer." He turned back to face Duffer. The man behind him also stared at him with a new found interest. "What is he suspected of doing?"

Per Agent Pruitt's request, Duffer could not leak information on the ongoing investigation. He had, however, developed a mutual respect relationship with the chief. He had to play it cool. "He's just a person of interest, I think. Maybe about damaging a hunting blind or something. I don't know any details."

Heathcock did not seem 100 percent convinced that there wasn't anything more, but he accepted the detective's response. "Okay. Thank you." His associate turned away, as if having lost interest in the interaction.

Driving back to Boydton, Nick spoke. "So, is that going to be an Indian reservation?"

"Well, just a territory for now. There are more items that need addressing to obtain reservation designation."

"Okay. That's kinda cool."

"Let me check the mail and then I'll take you home. I'll need to go in to the office for a while after that."

"That's fine. I want to start polishing some of the glass remnants in my rock tumbler anyway."

Detective Duffer found Dr. Hardy and Lucy standing in the post office when he arrived. He met them in the foyer.

"Hey, Doc. Lucy," he said.

"Hi, Bruce," said Hardy.

"My son, Nick here, just got back home. He was out West fighting the wildfires."

Nick nodded and smiled.

"Wow! That's great," said Hardy. "Those fires were massive."

"Yeah. That was a good thing to do," said Lucy. Nick and Bruce smiled in response to the praise.

"Yeah, I think so too. He recovered some pieces of molten glass to bring home."

"Oh, yeah?" said Hardy.

"Well," said Nick. "I'm gonna try to polish them. Like souvenirs."

"Neat," said Lucy. She added, "Oh, and Obie is getting his book published."

"Well, it's not being *published*. I'm just getting it printed," he said.

"Oh? What's it about?"

"Ah," said Hardy. "It's just a handbook of terms lay people use for medical terms. You know, like *high test hernia* for *hiatal hernia* and *Pepsi ulcer* for *peptic ulcer*."

"Oh, that sounds neat. Can't wait to see it."

"Maybe entertaining toilet reading, at least," said Hardy.

CHAPTER 30

FBI Agent Pruitt proved to be true to his word as Duffer received his weekly call on Monday, like clockwork. The detective took the call in his office.

"What's new in your investigation?" he asked.

"Well, we've found some new information on our Jay Zimmer," said Pruitt. "He's been spotted in New York state."

"New York? That's strange."

"Not exactly. You know that he likes hanging out with Native Americans. Well, there's an Iroquois reservation in that area."

"Oh. That is interesting," said the detective.

"And, there's more. Do you remember a death case you worked about six months ago? A Jon Griffin?"

"Hmm..." That name sounded familiar to Duffer. He thought for a moment. "Was that the man we found dead in the vacant store building?"

"Yep. Well, Jay Zimmer is his cousin."

"I think he was Native American, now that you mention it. But, there was nothing suspicious about that death that I recall."

"That's right. But he lived on an Iroquois reservation in New York state."

"I see. So, a little progress, huh?"

"Yeah. An odd connection. I'll let you know if anything else turns up. The FBI in New York has a BOLO out for him now. So, until next Monday or sooner."

"Sooner, I hope." *It seems like they're closing in on our prime suspect*, he thought. Hopefully, the FBI had found some concrete evidence incriminating this man. This all seemed like some extreme efforts in just acquiring some undeveloped land.

"Bruce, there's a call on line 1," came Betsy's voice over his speaker.

"Thanks, Betsy." He punched the phone button. "Duffer here."

"Bruce, it's Sidney Hudson. There's been an incident. I'm in the South Hill ER."

"Are you okay?"

"Not bad. Just getting some x-rays."

"I'm on my way."

Duffer discovered that his fellow officer had answered a domestic disturbance call in the Baskerville area. A male subject, apparently under the influence of drugs, alcohol, or both, had become violent. He resisted Hudson's arrest, and the two had fallen to the floor.

The detective found Sidney Hudson in ER room 9. He was sitting on a litter in a hospital gown, holding his right chest.

"How are you doing, Hudson?" he asked.

"Not too bad." He had a painful smile. "No rib fractures. Just bruised, we think."

"Sorry, man." Duffer had suffered from bruised ribs before and knew how uncomfortable this was and how long it took to recover.

"Thanks. It is in the job description, you know."

"Yeah. I hear you. What about the perp? Did you get him?"

"I was able to taze him, then cuffed him. We brought him in here. He's definitely flying high on something, though."

"Okay. I'll find the perp then come back here."

"Thanks."

Detective Duffer walked over to the work station, the hub of the ER. It was a rectangular corral area, fenced in by counters with computer terminals set up on them. The medical staff interacted here, sometimes in person, but more often digitally. Dr. Hardy approached him.

"I just saw a drunk who was tazed. Is he one of yours?" said the doctor.

"Afraid so. Resisting arrest. Is he okay to take away?"

"Well, his alcohol level is 243 and his CK is 1500. That shows some muscle damage. We'll hydrate him with a couple liters of IV fluid. I'll probably clear him in about two hours."

"Okay. I'll leave an officer to guard him till then."

"Fine. Oh, did your son do anything with those glass remnants?"

"Yeah. He put them in the tumbler for two to three days. Some are pretty-shaped, glossy jewels. He got some necklaces to mount them in."

"Hey. I've got a booth at the Holiday Bazaar this weekend. I'm trying to sell some of my booklets. It's a ten-foot vendor site. There's plenty of spare room if he wants to come and sell some, too."

"Yeah? That's a good idea. Thanks. I'll let him know."

He called in two deputies to guard the perp and provide another driver for Hudson's car. The nurse rolled Hudson out to Duffer's car by wheelchair.

"I'm okay. Is this really necessary?" said Hudson.

"Yes," answered Duffer. "You shouldn't drive with bruised ribs yet. Especially a county vehicle!"

"And we gave you pain medication," added the nurse.

"Thanks," said Duffer.

As they drove back to the sheriff's office, Hudson began a conversation.

"Anything new on your murder case?"

"Well, the suspect's been spotted in New York state. We'll see what comes out of it."

"At least there's a lead."

"Yeah."

After work, Duffer called his son. Nick had returned to Petersburg over the weekend. He had sent Duffer pictures of his fire gems on his phone. They were like jewels, smooth and sparkling.

"Dr. Hardy told me he has a vendor's booth booked at the Holiday Bazaar this weekend. He's offered you some space if you want to try to sell some of your jewelry."

"Oh, yeah? That would be awesome! Thanks."

CHAPTER 31

The Holiday Bazaar is a local fundraising event hosted annually by the South Hill library. It is usually their largest fundraiser of the year. It was set in a tobacco warehouse, now nearly empty following the storage and marketing of the season's crop. There was a distinct lingering scent of tobacco, but it was overpowered by the aroma of the Brunswick stew cooking. Dr. Hardy's booth was on the corner of one of the aisles. A six-foot folding table marked the site where number 41 was chalked on the floor. He had a poster of his book cover, *Street Talk Medical Guide*, on display. Hardy had a box of paperback booklets with some placed in small stacks on the table.

Nick was carrying a small plastic storage box when he found Dr. Hardy. He was now clean shaven.

"Hey, Nick. Welcome," said Dr. Hardy. "I see you lost your beard."

"Yeah. I'm back to civilization now. Hey, thanks for the invite." Nick looked all around. Booths of Christmas decorations, candles, crafts, and baked goods spread out over the thirty-thousand-square-foot warehouse. "Wow! This is great!"

"Yeah, it is. I brought a small card table if you need one," said Hardy.

"Great." He began unfolding the table and opened up his plastic box. He placed a small poster on the table. In bold print it read: **Fire Drops** with a brief note describing their origin. It stated that sales proceeds went to support the National Fire Protection Association. "I only brought twenty-two pendants," he said. "I haven't had time to polish more than that yet."

Hardy looked over the unusual jewels. "These look great," he said.

A good crowd was in attendance to support the event, easily numbering in the thousands. Visitors ambled along the aisles, studying the diverse wares. A young lady with medium-length hair and tall boots closely inspected a fire drop necklace.

"Some of these take on a hazy, smoky look," explained Nick. "And others are peppered with specks of ash. They give these gems a unique character and authenticity."

"Oh, I see," she said. "I like them a lot."

"It kind of sheds a new light on 'smoky' topaz stones."

"Yeah," she laughed.

She became his first customer. The jewelry was well received by the bazaar patrons, and by noon, he had sold a dozen necklaces.

"I think I'll get a hamburger," said Nick. "You want something too?"

"Yeah," said Hardy. He handed him a five. "A barbecue and a drink. Thanks. I'll watch out over your stuff."

"Okay."

After lunch, they took tag-team toilet breaks, keeping the booth attended at all times. Dr. Hardy had sold fifteen to twenty books. Many local friends and some of his patients had stopped by the booth. He recognized another familiar person as they approached.

"Bruce," he greeted as the detective walked up. "Good to see you."

"Doc. Is Nick here giving you any trouble?" said Duffer.

"Are you kidding? He's close to selling out."

"Well, I'm not doing too bad," said Nick modestly.

"Good. I was just here to check on you guys," said Duffer. Suddenly, his cell phone rang. "Hello … Agent Pruitt?" He walked off a few steps, seeking some privacy. As the conversation proceeded, Duffer appeared to become happy. After the call, he rejoined the salesmen and Nick spoke.

"Business call?"

"Yeah," said Duffer. He turned to Dr. Hardy. "Do you remember the explosion at the solar test site?"

"Yeah. Suspected arson and possible murder," said Hardy.

"The FBI just arrested our prime suspect ... in New York state."

CHAPTER 32

Jay Zimmer was being held in the city jail of Olean, New York. The biggest obstacle in his extrication was physically transporting him to Mecklenburg County, five hundred miles south. To expedite this process, the US Marshall's office commissioned some county officers for the job. Detective Duffer teamed with Sidney Hudson for the prisoner transfer. Sidney was still recuperating from his rib injury, but eight hours of a road trip would be less strenuous than running calls.

They drove a county cruiser on the journey up through Pennsylvania via Washington, DC. The route was along interstates until halfway through Pennsylvania where they picked up State Route 155 up to Olean. They made a refueling break at a truck stop, and the two officers walked into the dining area.

"I thought we could grab some lunch here," said Duffer.

"Sure," said Sidney. "But what's with all this country music you've got on the radio?"

"What do you mean?"

"You know black folks don't listen to that country crap." He was smiling at Duffer.

"Well, they're black country singers, too."

"Really? Who?"

"Well…like…Darius Rucker."

"Okay. That's one."

"So, what do you listen to?"

"You know, rap and maybe some R&B."

"Rap? Are you from the streets? Like *Hudson from the hood*?"

"Ow!" said Hudson. He grabbed his right chest area like he'd been stabbed. "Don't make me laugh. It hurts!"

"Okay. Let's say the driver chooses the radio station. Fair enough?"

"Yeah. It's a deal."

It was dark by the time they reached Olean. It was a small city along Interstate 86, the county seat of Cattaraugus County. The Allegany Indian Reservation extended from Allegany County into Cattaraugus County. It was a large reservation, over thirty thousand acres with a population of 823. They found a Quality Inn and checked in. There was a pizza restaurant just a block away, and they walked over to it.

"A cold beer would go good with this pizza," said Sidney.

"Go ahead, if you want. I don't drink myself. Just don't put it on the county's account."

"Oh, no problem. I still have some pain pills left. If I needed one, I wouldn't want to mix it with alcohol."

"Makes sense."

The aroma of cheese and pepperonis was delightful as their order arrived. They wasted no time in starting the meal.

"Would this be New-York-style pizza?" asked Sidney.

"Well, I guess, technically, it is," said Duffer.

As they began to eat, Sidney spoke. "So, this Zimmer guy, did he kill that dude?"

"I think so," said Duffer. "But the evidence is mostly circumstantial at this point." He believed Zimmer was involved in the kidnapping, too. But there was no hard proof of that either. *He's a crafty weasel,* he thought.

"Were there any security cameras at the solar energy site?"

"Well, yes. But they were aimed at the solar panel field. Nothing was recorded in the shed."

"That's a bad break, huh?"

"Yeah. We'll need to rest up tonight. It's a long drive tomorrow."

"I know that."

At 6:00 AM, they arose to get an early start. It was a cold morning, dusted lightly with snow that had crept in overnight. They easily found the police station on East Street. It was a two-story building of tan-colored brick with large windows. Duffer presented the receptionist with the US Marshall's prisoner transfer order. She escorted them promptly to a back office.

"Sergeant Harold, these officers are here for a prisoner transfer," she said to a uniformed man. He looked over the papers and spoke.

"Okay, Officers. Just wait here. I'll be back with this Jay Zimmer."

In no time at all, he had returned with a hand-and-ankle-cuffed male in an orange jumpsuit.

"Better watch this one," said Sergeant Harold. "We picked him up out near the rez. He's not a member of any tribe. He was wearing a bear skin over his back. Just an Indian groupie, I guess."

"Sounds about right," said Duffer. "Thanks."

They placed a coat over Zimmer's prison attire. His eyes were dark and sunken, a bit eerie as he moved mechanically out with the detective. As Duffer loaded the prisoner into the caged-off back seat, he had a feeling that this was anticlimactic, just routine procedure. He felt that this did not neatly tie up the case. Why would a nontribal member go to the extremes of kidnapping, sabotage, and murder to help the Indians obtain a property? The waters were still murky on this case. He would have to wait for the chance to interrogate him in Virginia.

Well into Pennsylvania, Duffer thought he might get some clues with some general conversation.

"I guess you know that Jon Griffin died," he said. Zimmer just stared out the side window in silence. "Wasn't he your cousin?"

After a pause and with no eye contact, Zimmer said flatly, "Yeah."

"Did he want the Weyanoke tribe to get the land in Mecklenburg County?"

Zimmer was obviously not in the mood for conversation. He sat apathetically in the rear seat. His response was delayed. "He wanted the tribe to get the land."

Duffer realized the approach of discussing his cousin was not opening him up. He decided to refrain from pressing for more direct information on the case. The detective was aware of the need to interrogate him in the proper manner, under Miranda notice and recorded. He didn't want to give him any previews that would allow him to formulate his responses.

Deputy Hudson also made an attempt to get Zimmer to speak with an unrelated query. They were eighty-six miles north of DC. "So, how do you feel about ditching the Washington Redskins' mascot?"

His question was ignored by the prisoner. Duffer offered his opinion.

"Well, game days pack the stadium, and there are waiting lists for tickets. Thousands of fans wave foam tomahawks and wear face paint. It seems incredibly popular."

Still no response from the back seat.

"Imitation is the sincerest form of flattery," added Hudson. "Is it that the term *redskins* is supposed to be offensive?"

No opinion was offered from their prisoner.

"To me," said Duffer, "it would depend on the context. I mean, like … if you call someone a rascal, it can mean a heartless scoundrel, or, like, a playful fella. As a national football team mascot, I think *Redskins* is more like a term of endearment."

"Yeah. Me too," said Hudson.

Somewhere in northern Virginia their tight-lipped passenger began tapping his fingers against the side door. *Pum-pum-pump, pum-pum-pump.* Duffer froze. That beat sounded too familiar to him. *Yes!* he thought. It was the same beat he had heard on Phillip Merit's phone. Was this a coincidence?

During their trip, they used the interstate rest areas' toilet facilities. This avoided handling a shackled prisoner in private businesses. Even including a few fast-food stops, they were able to deliver their captive cargo to the Mecklenburg County jail by five thirty. The final part of their mission was to retrieve their vehicles parked at the sheriff's office. As they were unloading their overnight bags from the trunk, a man walked out from the front entrance. Duffer recognized Logan Dalton from the lumber company.

"Hey, Mr. Dalton," he greeted.

Mr. Dalton did not pause to chat. He muttered "Detective," bluntly as he walked briskly away.

Hmm, thought Duffer. *I wonder what that's all about.*

CHAPTER 33

Dr. Hardy breathed in the hearty aroma from his morning coffee mug. He took sips as he chewed on a bagel, perusing the weekly local paper. It was 1:00 AM when he had made it to bed, coming home from the evening ER shift at eleven. Lucy was seated in the adjoining family room watching the morning news. An occurrence from the evening's work shift came to his mind.

"Lucy. I had an unusual case last night."

"Oh, yeah? Another overdose?"

"No. It was a twenty-four-year-old girl who came in feeling queasy. She was taking Menopur, a fertility drug, and had taken a dose the night before. I checked a pregnancy test and a urinalysis that were normal. I thought it was just a side effect of her medication. I offered her some nausea medicine but she declined."

"So, what's so interesting about that?"

"Well, after getting home, she called back to the ER. I took the call and talked to her again, suggesting things to try for nausea and reducing or skipping her Menopur dose. Then, five minutes later, she called back again and asked specifically to speak to *the nurse*."

"You're kidding."

"She finally told the nurse the real problem. Apparently, she had performed oral sex on her husband the day before and spit out his load into a half-empty water bottle at the bedside. Then, the next day, she inadvertently took a swallow from the bottle."

"Ewh!"

"Yeah. The nurse was punching herself in the thigh to keep from laughing over the phone. She turned to me after the call and said 'I guess that's like a *snowball!*'"

"What's a snowball?"

"Ah, you better look it up in the Urban Dictionary. I did."

Lucy googled on her phone and, after a brief pause, cried out, "Oh! That's just gross!"

"You can't make this stuff up. But, you know, if she is taking fertility drugs to get pregnant, oral sex isn't the best way to conceive."

Hardy took another sip of coffee. Somehow, it didn't taste quite as good as it had before. Looking back to his newspaper, the front-page lead story caught his attention.

"Hey, Lucy. Did you see this about the riverboat?"

"Yeah. I think so," she said.

"The Wyanoke site, on Mitchell Road, has put in a request with the Corps of Engineers for a riverboat."

"Uh-huh," she said.

"That's a neat idea! I guess it could be like the Annabelle Lee in Richmond, a paddle wheel boat with a taste of colonial America from the 1880s. Only on the Roanoke River instead of the James."

Lucy looked up from her cell phone. "But the Annabelle Lee cruised to the James River plantations. What would this one do?"

"Well, there's the Elm Hill plantation house. Lady Jean Skipwith lived there. She later married Sir Peyton Skipwith, the Baronet of Prestwood. You can still see her plantation house from the dam."

"Oh, yeah. I know that house."

"I guess they could have a dinner cruise, maybe with a band or a Native American dance show. Even events, like weddings and anniversary bookings."

"That could be a business stream for the Indians."

"Yeah. I think it's neat."

"I could see tourist buses coming in for that."

"Uh-huh."

The next page had the Mecklenburg County police report along with an ad for storage units. "Hey! They arrested the guy who may have sabotaged the solar energy test site. He was captured in New York state."

"Why did he sabotage the test site?"

"I guess he was trying to run off RAE so the Indians might get that land."

"You know, it's the twenty-first century now, and Indians and progressive business developers are still fighting over American land. That's sad!"

Detective Duffer met with FBI Agent Pruitt at the sheriff's office the day after the prisoner transport. They had prepared a room for Zimmer's interrogation. Stanley, the public defense attorney, was present as his counsel.

"I'd like to take the lead on this," Pruitt said to Duffer.

Duffer was holding his investigation file in preparation. It had taken the resources of the FBI to hunt down the suspect. And, the kidnapping was actually out of Virginia state's jurisdiction, in North Carolina. It was only fair. "Yes, sir. Sure."

The room was bare except for a centrally positioned table and four chairs. A recorder was set up on the table, and Jay Zimmer was seated beside his attorney. The two officers sat down on the opposite side, and Duffer switched on the recorder.

"Mr. Zimmer," said Pruitt, "you've been charged with felony kidnapping and first-degree murder. We would like you to have an opportunity to share your thoughts about these charges. They are very serious."

The public defender spoke. "Mr. Zimmer, you don't have to say anything. If there is something that may confirm your innocence, you may consider telling it."

Zimmer looked at the defender, then gazed down at the table.

After pausing for a response, Pruitt continued. "You were employed by RAE solar power company from July to November. Is that correct?"

Without raising his head, he spoke softly, "Yes." He did not elaborate.

"As an employee, were you given access to the test site on Mitchell Road?"

A very flat "Yes" was offered.

"What equipment was housed at this site?"

After some hesitation, the suspect responded. "Basically, a modulator, storage batteries, and an AC inverter."

Agent Pruitt looked at Detective Duffer, as if inviting his input at this time. He had, nonetheless, been to the scene when the RAE engineer made his analysis.

"Mr. Zimmer," asked Duffer. "Can you tell us what would happen if there was a leak in the battery casing?"

"I don't know. Maybe a fire hazard or something."

Duffer sensed that he was truly not aware of the severity of this action.

Agent Pruitt injected, "Did you drill holes in those battery casings?"

"You don't have to answer that!" the public defender said promptly.

Zimmer looked at his attorney and then gave Pruitt a blank gaze. He said nothing. Pruitt, having met a road block, paused to regroup. "Ah… Mr. Zimmer," he began, "were you aware of the protesters at the site on Mitchell Road?"

"The tree hugger? Yeah."

"Did you know that he was kidnapped?"

"I'm not surprised," he responded.

"What do you mean by that?"

"That property is protected by spirits. Ancient native burial grounds are there."

"And you think these *evil spirits* took that man?"

"I wouldn't be surprised. Sometimes the shape-shifters do their work." As he stared eerily at his interrogators, his eyes appeared dark, almost black, not exactly human. Duffer turned his gaze to Stanley, the public defender, and felt that he was just as perplexed over this revelation.

Jay Zimmer was done speaking and answered no further questions. He was returned to his jail cell as Pruitt and Duffer conferred in Duffer's office cubicle.

"So, what do you think?" asked Pruitt.

"Well, first of all, I'm not sure he was aware that a hydrogen leak would lead to an explosion. I don't know if he's that knowledgeable. I'm wondering if he just meant to cause a fire."

"Yeah. Sabotage and murder. But, if he wasn't smart enough, maybe not a premeditated murder, but an accidental murder. Still, this case is largely circumstantial at this point."

"I agree. And he's pulling this *voo-doo* shit about evil spirits and the kidnapping. We're no further along than before. But he did state that it was a native burial ground. That implies that he knew about the skull and bones that were planted there. We never released that info since it's still an active investigation."

"Yeah. Maybe we can link it somehow. Still, what's his motive? He's not a member of any tribe, and to work this hard to help them obtain some land …"

"I know." Duffer wondered if Heathcock might shed some light on this. "I think I'll have a chat with Chief Heathcock. To get an insider's perspective."

"That's good. Thanks for your help."

"Oh, Pruitt," said Duffer suddenly. He had been curious about seeing Dalton there the evening before. "I saw Logan Dalton, the timber man, here yesterday. Do you know anything about that?"

"Yeah. I saw in your report about how he knew about the solar site sabotage and seemed eager to capitalize on it, even before it was public."

"Yes. I thought that was a bit odd too."

"Seems that his employee, with his rescue-squad friend, has permission to hunt on that property. He's out there frequently. Wouldn't be much left to hunt if it were covered by solar panels."

"Oh, I see. Is he a suspect, you think?"

"Well, a person of interest for now."

CHAPTER 34

Chief Heathcock agreed to speak with Detective Duffer again that afternoon. Duffer had his car radio on as he drove out to Heathcock's office. He was oblivious to the music being broadcast as he mulled over the details of the cases, formulating his theories.

As he entered the administrative office of the Wyanoake, he met a gentleman who was leaving. It was a tall, slender man with a ponytail, the same man he had seen at the new site on Mitchell Road.

"Good day, Officer," he said politely to Duffer.

"You too," Duffer replied with a nod.

Heathcock stepped out from his office and waved Duffer in. "Hello, Detective. Come on in."

"Thanks."

"So, what's going on with you?"

"Well, Chief. I guess you know that Jay Zimmer has been arrested."

"Yes, I've heard that. What has he done?"

"He's charged with sabotage and probably murder at the solar test site. And he's a suspect in the kidnapping." He felt he could trust Heathcock's discretion.

"Oh. That's serious stuff. He seemed like a drifter. But not like someone who would be driven to do these crimes."

"Yeah, I know. I just can't see his motivation."

"Me either."

Nothing more useful was offered. Duffer continued. "You know, he blames it on evil spirits. He called them *shape-shifters*."

Chief Heathcock's face froze in a most serious expression. He was dramatically silent. Duffer sensed there was more to this and pressed. "Does this mean something to you?"

"Shape-shifters are evil, like black magic. They are witches, often walking on all fours, and are reported to have the ability to change their form into that of an animal. They portray such evil that just mentioning their name is believed to conjure up bad happenings. Many will wear the skins of that animal on their backs. Hence, they are called..." He looks around and leans forward, lowering his voice, "the *skin walkers*."

His words caused Duffer to feel a chill run down his spine. "When he was arrested, they reported that he was wearing a bear skin and acting oddly."

Heathcock looked away, pondering what he had heard before turning back to Duffer. "Our medicine men harness the powers of good. Some practitioners become driven by powers to do harm. If they follow this path of evil, they could ultimately become a skin walker. This is most prevalent in Navajo tribes. Native Americans rarely speak of them out of fear that they might invite evil events."

"Do you think Zimmer could have become one of these skin walkers?" Duffer wasn't even certain if he even possessed any actual Native American heritage.

"It's possible, but one doesn't need the supernatural just to be evil. The transformation from an evil sorcerer to a full-powered shape-shifter requires a horrendous act. Often, it is the killing of someone close to them, usually a family member. Once the crossover occurs, there is no returning of the soul."

"So, what's your take on the Mitchell Road land? Is it cursed by evil spirits or just evil people?"

"I regret that the acquisition of our land has been clouded by such tragedy. We have found no evidence to substantiate a native burial site. Evil spirits? I can't really say."

"Well, thanks for your help, Chief."

As he drove home, Duffer thought, *More smoke but no fire.* He mulled over Chief Heathcock's recounting of the skin walkers– "... killing of someone close," "...a family member."

"Jon Griffin!" he suddenly thought aloud. *He was Zimmer's cousin. That death was deemed natural causes. But what if it wasn't?*

CHAPTER 35

It was Friday afternoon when Dr. Hardy and Lucy were out at the horse farm. It was mid-December but a mild fifty degrees with light gray clouds smothering the sky. They were preparing to ride two of the horses back to the new pasture at their house, two miles away.

"If you get the saddles out, I'll get the bridles," said Lucy.

"Okay. Thanks," said Hardy sarcastically. The pair of saddles far outweighed her share of the tack. They toted their gear to the round pen where the horses were corralled. Dr. Hardy's cell phone rang, halting his preparations.

As he hung up, Lucy asked, "Who was that?"

"An ME case. The other side of South Hill." They both looked at the horses, frustrated by this intrusion, and turned back to the tack room.

At 4:15 PM, there was at most an hour of daylight remaining, adding some urgency to his response. This case interrupted Dr. Hardy's day off, sending him racing to a street address off Route 1. He turned onto Oak Leaf Road and found himself on a curving, graveled tar road. He slowed down, partly due to the dangerous turns but also since he was searching for the address he was given. His destination was marked by the red flashing lights of two EMS vehicles and the emergency flashers of a Crown Victoria. This was in a particularly sharp turn bordered by large trees. He parked and was met by Detective Duffer.

"Hey, Doc. Our body is over here." He gestured off to their left. "Ejected from the vehicle, thrown about fifty feet."

That seemed like a deadly scenario. As they started off in that direction, they walked past a tree with a mass of mangled metal wrapped around it. The bark was freshly marred, and the smell of steam and hot motor oil hung in the air.

"Is that the car?" said Hardy. It was barely recognizable as automotive scrap.

"Well, the front end," said Duffer. He pointed further off to the left. There was the rear half of a gray SUV lying on its side.

"Oh my God! It's split in two?"

"Yep. Apparently, he was traveling at an excessive speed, not advisable on this road. He was late to pick up his daughter from his ex-in-laws."

"Oh. That's bad. At least she wasn't riding with him."

"Yeah. The only good thing."

The body was lying prone with the arms twisted in unnatural positions. He was a Caucasian male appearing in his midthirties. Hardy gloved up and placed a meat thermometer in the man's armpit.

"What happened to your porch thermometer?" said Duffer.

"I upgraded. The central office in Richmond uses these."

He proceeded with his external exam, beginning with palpation of the cranium. A fracture to the right frontoparietal skull was palpable. In addition, there was a fracture of the right clavicle and several ribs on the right chest.

"These are obviously fatal injuries. He'll just need a blood alcohol level and toxicologies," said Hardy.

"It's okay for the funeral home then?"

"Yeah. I'll call it in to Richmond." He pulled out a syringe and vial from his ME bag.

"Good." Duffer paused as if mulling over something as Dr. Hardy pulled up a syringe of dark burgundy blood from the man's subclavian vein. "Say, Doc. What do you know about psychiatry?"

"Well, a passing knowledge, I guess. Is it for you or do you have a *friend* who's crazy?"

"I'm not sure. Is there some condition that would make someone believe that they were something like a werewolf or a demon?"

Dr. Hardy thought about multiple personality disorder. Duffer's description, however, sounded like a more disturbed condition. He emptied the syringe of blood into the vial.

"I guess a schizoaffective disorder could have those manifestations. It's bordering on schizophrenia. More have paranoid types of delusions, but some exhibit grandiosity."

"Hmm. That's something that I might work with."

"Again, this isn't my area of expertise. So, what's this about anyway, if I might ask?"

"Oh, I've got this suspect who thinks he's an Indian demon or something. I'm not sure that he is competent."

"Doesn't sound like it."

The daylight was waning, intensifying the red ambulance lights and the yellow flashing of the tow truck that was pulling up. As the truck backed its rollback trailer toward the wreckage, a loud roaring began, accenting the back-up beeping warning. Over the noise, Dr. Hardy waved goodbye to Detective Duffer.

CHAPTER 36

Duffer discovered a large object on the ground ahead. The identity was obscured by a haze. He approached cautiously. The fogginess was clearing as he drew near. It was a human body that appeared blackened, burnt. Trails of smoke arising from the body formed the fog.

He hears some growling and sees that an animal, a wolf or maybe a bear, is gnawing on the man's arm. A rhythmic beat arises.

Pum-pum pump ... pum-pum pump.

The animal turns its head to face Duffer and jumps back away from the body. The beating intensifies.

Pum-pum pump! Pum-pum pump!

The animal's face appears to be human. As Duffer focuses on the face, and it grows clearer. It is Jay Zimmer!

Duffer bolted up in bed! He was chilled but covered in sweat. His pulse was pounding in his head.

Pump... pump... pump ... pump!

"Bruce? Are you okay?" came Ann's voice.

He looked about the bedroom. His breathing was rapid.

"Ah...yeah. I'm okay," he answered. "Just a bad dream." He wondered if all this talk about the skin walkers had cursed his sleep.

The following morning, Duffer asked Agent Pruitt to stop by his office cubicle. He shared with him what he had learned from Chief Heathcock.

"And, take a look at this." Duffer pulled up a file on his computer. A black-and-white surveillance-type video popped onto the screen "This is the security footage at Occoneechee State Park the night that the skull was stolen."

"Yeah. I've seen it. Just a couple of animals in the parking lot."

Duffer froze the picture with a large mammal in view. "Look at his legs." The fur appeared unattached to the legs, flopping loosely over limbs that seemed too small. "I think this is a person with an animal skin over his body!"

"No. You're not serious about this *skin walker* spiel, are you?"

"Well, Zimmer was wearing a bear skin when he was arrested. What if he *thinks* he is a skin walker? He steals the skull, plants it in the fake burial site, kidnaps Phillip Merit, and sabotages the RAE test site."

"Because he's some evil sorcerer?"

"Well, if he *believes* he is."

Pruitt still looked skeptical. "I don't know, Bruce. This ghost and spirit shit is way out there. Do you want us to take this hocus-pocus stuff to court?"

"I don't know. I'm just saying …" He added, "Maybe he needs a psych eval anyway."

"Well, I can't disagree with that."

He hoped Pruitt didn't think that he, himself, needed a psych as well. Betsy's voice on the speaker phone interrupted them. "Detective Duffer. Bill Bradson is here to see you. It seems urgent."

"Okay, show him back." He turned to Pruitt. "He's the realtor who worked out the deal on the Mitchell property."

Bradson rushed over to them. "Bruce, you might wanna see this!" He dropped a sheet of paper on Duffer's desk.

"What?" He looked down at the document. It was a request for a state permit from the Richmond office.

"Gambling!" said Bradson. "The Wyanoake have requested a gambling permit for their riverboat!"

"Are you serious? A riverboat casino?"

"Yep. This copy was filed with the county board of supervisors."

"So," said Pruitt, "they requested a commercial riverboat approval from the Corps of Engineers for a tourist attraction. And now, a gaming permit from the state gaming commission?"

"That's right, ah …" Bradson looked at him inquisitively.

"Pruitt, FBI Agent Pruitt," he said. He turned to the detective. "Bruce, looks like your Indian Chief has been holding out on us, huh?"

"It would seem so," said Duffer. This could certainly make that land project worth fighting over.

"I know a little about Native American casinos," said Pruitt. "There are over four hundred gambling facilities in twenty-eight states. They gross over $26 billion annually. That's more than Las Vegas and Atlantic City combined. It's legal in any state that has legalized gambling."

"Do the states get a portion of the revenues?" asked Duffer. He was trying to see a positive side to this.

"Well, it's negotiable. The states can't 'tax' tribal income since reservations are not US properties. But they can collect 'permit fees' and like a 'cover charge' per gambler."

"Can I keep this copy, Bill?"

"Sure, Bruce. That one's for you."

"Thanks for bringing this by," said Duffer.

As Bradson left, Pruitt spoke. "We need to talk to your chief friend again."

The following day, Evelyn Gates arrived at the sheriff's office. She was the FBI forensic psychiatrist. Her brown hair was in a bun, giving her the look of an elementary school matron. Her black-rimmed glasses gave the illusion of possessing a keen, focused insight, able to penetrate anyone's shell. Duffer and Pruitt escorted her to the interrogation room where she was to evaluate Jay Zimmer.

"I see you have Zimmer's file," said Agent Pruitt.

"Yes. I studied it last night to get a picture of his background," she answered. "He seems to be a muddled piece of work."

"Yeah, for sure. We hope you can shed some light on this case for us," said Pruitt.

"No promises, but I'll give it a shot."

As she entered the room, he closed the door behind her. He and Detective Duffer positioned themselves behind the observation mirror to watch. Zimmer appeared as his distant, tight-lipped self, as if in some weird trance. Betsy interrupted them.

"Excuse me, Detective, but Chief Heathcock is here."

"Thanks, Betsy," said Duffer. "Show him into the meeting room."

"All right."

Heathcock had agreed to come by the sheriff's office that morning. The detective and Pruitt joined him in a private conference room.

"Detective Duffer," he said lightheartedly. "We have to stop meeting like this."

"Yeah, I know, Chief," said Duffer. "I think you know Agent Pruitt from the FBI."

"Yes. How may I help you gentlemen? I've told you all I know about Jay Zimmer."

"Well," said Pruitt, "we understand that your tribe is planning to open a Native American casino on your newly acquired land."

Heathcock appeared to be taken aback. He bowed his head solemnly before looking up to speak. He began slowly. "It was not my intention to seek to start a gambling operation on this beautiful property. We sought to develop a Native American haven, a new homeland for our people. The riverboat project offered an opportunity to financially support our mission."

"So, you hadn't intended to have gambling on board?" Agent Pruitt said.

"That's correct."

"So, what changed?" asked Pruitt.

Heathcock took a pensive pause, appearing to search for the best response. "A financial consultant, who had worked with several large tribes in the Midwest, approached us. He helped us procure the Mitchell Road property. Oh, incidentally, we decided to name it Roanoke Shores."

"For the Roanoke River," said Duffer. It seemed like a good name, bringing in the river's name and not including a label like "Indian." "I like that."

"And this financial consultant," asked Pruitt, "did he influence the development of Roanoke Shores?"

"Yes," said Heathcock somberly. "I signed off on all the forms and applications. I now see that I should have read them more carefully."

There was an abrupt knock at the door.

"Agent Pruitt?" came the voice of Evelyn Gates.

"Yes. Come in," he replied.

"I've uncovered something I thought that you'd need to know. Mr. Zimmer has schizoaffective disorder… but it seems that he was taken advantage of."

"What do you mean?" asked Duffer. This seemed to fit his theory.

"Well, he's been obsessed with joining an Indian tribe for years. Someone led him to believe that he was becoming a skin walker, an evil Native American sorcerer. He was so encouraged that he came to assume this identity."

"But why?" asked Duffer.

"So that he would become a true Native American."

That seemed like an awful initiation ritual. He had been exploited, capitalizing on his mental illness.

"That's incredible," said Agent Pruitt. "Did he give you the name of this person?"

"Yes. He said it was—"

"Isaac Norton," interjected Chief Heathcock.

CHAPTER 37

FBI Agent Pruitt stood beside Detective Duffer's desk holding several pages of paper.

"Chief Heathcock says this Isaac Norton traveled here from South Dakota," said Duffer.

"Yes. I've run a profile on him," said Pruitt. He laid a photo on Duffer's desk. "Here's a visual, although it's a couple of years old." It was a black-and-white photo of a man with Native American or, possibly, Hispanic features—dark skin, straight black hair. "He has connections with the Native Mob."

"The Native Mob?" asked Duffer. *How extensive does this reach?* He thought.

"Yeah. It's an organized crime network that originated in the 1990s. Originally, it was in Minnesota, Wisconsin, and South Dakota."

"Well, we had some MS 13 in this area a few years ago. They were involved in a cockfighting operation."

"Yeah? Well, the Native Mob usually deals with drugs and robberies. Casinos have given them a super opportunity to grow."

"How big is this Native Mob?"

"We believe there are about 1,500 members in all now. Not huge, but significant ranks. I've put out a warrant for Norton's arrest in South Dakota."

"Good! I hope we can nip this thing in the bud. Small, rural communities like ours shouldn't have to worry with gangs and mobsters," said Duffer.

"Well, no place is immune to crime gangs nowadays."

Duffer felt like Heathcock had played the part of a pawn in this game. He had always been forthcoming and cooperative with the detective. Maybe he hadn't wanted to believe that Isaac Norton's motives were not virtuous and that he might be scheming to expand his gambling empire.

"So, we take Zimmer to trial," said Duffer.

"Absolutely! And I'll continue the search for this Isaac Norton."

CHAPTER 38

The first week of spring proved to be cool, in the low sixties, but sunny. Roanoke Shores, the Native American territory, had just launched their paddle-wheel boat, *River Spirit*. The sixty-foot vessel was mounted on pontoons with a two-story paddle wheel on the stern. Although entirely decorative, the wheel was designed to turn as the ship moved along the waters. The main deck level had a bar to the rear and a small stage toward the bow. A man sat at a piano-style keyboard up front playing saloon-style music. The second level had the captain's house and a partially covered observation deck.

Detective Duffer and Ann were boarding the vessel with Agent Pruitt. They had taken up Chief Heathcock on his invitation to visit. The chief was wearing a feathered headpiece and stood at the gangplank walkway.

"Welcome aboard the *River Spirit*," he said, as Detective Duffer approached with his party.

"Thanks, Chief," said Duffer. "You know Agent Pruitt, and this is my wife, Ann."

"Pleased to meet you. Now, everyone, find yourself a good seat."

The seating was bench style, facing forward, with small table sections at intervals in front of the rows. A pair of spiral stairs were near the center, leading up to the upper level. On top, the fore half was covered, leaving the rear deck open. White metal railings lined the outer edges of the riverboat with windowed walls enclosing the lower level. Two tall smoke stacks towered above the boat.

As they looked for some seats, Duffer saw someone seated across the deck waving to him.

"Hey, Bruce. Come on over," called Dr. Hardy. He was seated toward the rear with his wife.

"Dr. Hardy, Lucy," said Duffer, "this is FBI Agent Pruitt. Fancy meeting you here."

"Obie's talked about this project for months," said Lucy. "We just had to come see it for ourselves."

"It's a fantastic rig," said Duffer.

"I want to go upstairs," said Lucy.

"Oh, I'll go with you," said Ann.

"Is that one of Nick's fire drop necklaces?" she asked.

"Yes, it is," replied Ann proudly as they walked off.

"This land dispute sure seemed to work out for the best," said Dr. Hardy.

"Yeah. I like the Wyanoake tribe here," said Duffer.

"Say, whatever happened with that tree-sitter kidnapping?"

"We think Jay Zimmer was one of the perpetrators. And, also, responsible for the RAE test site sabotage."

"Really? But I didn't think he was convicted."

"Not guilty by reason of insanity," stated Agent Pruitt.

"Oh, man! What a bummer!" said Hardy.

"Yeah. A nightmare," said Duffer. "But we identified the instigator of all that crap."

"Isaac Norton," added Pruitt.

"Oh. And what happened to him?" asked Hardy.

"The FBI determined that he's left the country," said Duffer.

"Where to?" asked Hardy.

"Mexico," answered Pruitt.

"So he got away with it too?" said Hardy.

Agent Pruitt had a twinkle in his eye as a sly smile crept across his face. "Well, we've tracked him down in Oaxaca, Mexico."

"Where's that?" asked Hardy.

"It's a rugged territory in southwestern Mexico. It's largely populated by indigenous people, probably descendants of the Aztec."

"Why do you think he would have gone there?" asked Duffer.

"Native people, casinos," stated Pruitt.

Bronk … bronk sounded the boat's horns as the gangway was pulled ashore. The motors began to roar, the paddle wheels started turning, and the *River Spirit* eased out across the water.

Dr. Hardy ME mysteries

Carnal Deeds

Episode 5
Dr. Hardy ME Mysteries

Chapter 1

Dr. Hardy peered into the microscope lens examining an ER patient's test swab. He rotated the 400 X objective, clicked it in place and adjusted the focus. The foggy visual field sharpened to reveal quivering tear-shaped organisms. They resembled a cluster of balloons, tossed about in the wind, their beating flagellae were like trailing strings.

"Well, hello," he said to himself. "It's trichomonas." It seemed bad enough for a 16-year old girl to be subjected to her first pelvic exam by an unfamiliar doctor in an emergency room. But, now, Dr. Hardy must break the news to her that she has a STD.

"Dr. Hardy," called out the unit secretary. "The ME's office is on line two."

"Thanks." He pushed the flashing button and picked up the desk phone. "Dr. Hardy here."

"Are you available for an ME case?" asked the investigator. Dr, Hardy was one of the four county Medical Examiners, local appointees of the Office of the Chief Medical Examiner (OCME) in Richmond. That office was 90 miles away so local MEs would help with the necessary forensics.

"I get off in about an hour. Where is it?"

"Beechwood Acres, on Ebony Hill Road. Draper Funeral Home can transport the body to their funeral home. You can view the body there."

"Okay. I'll give them a call when I get off."

"Oh, be sure to get a urine specimen for toxicology. This is a suspected OD."

He hung up the phone, drew in a deep breath, and proceeded to exam room seven with the STD message. Surprisingly, she was almost amused when he told her.

"Oh! So that's what it is?" She smiled and added, "So, I'm not pregnant?"

"No. But I've sent tests off for the other common sexually transmitted diseases. Those results will be back in 24 hours. Would you like to take an antibiotic for those as well, just in case?"

"No, thanks. I'll just wait for the results."

Dr. Hardy walked out to his work station, shaking his head. At age 58, he had worked in this community hospital ER for over 20 years. Despite its rural location, the South Hill ER was quite busy. It was in the only actual city in this agricultural county. Initially, he had been able to dictate his notes and transcriptionists would type up the record that he would sign some time later. He had practiced through the birth and evolution of electronic health records. Despite this, his computer skills were still rudimentary. In this day and age, to practice medicine, he had to be a secretary, a data entry technician and a billing coder.

At 6:45 PM, Dr. Hardy called Draper Funeral Home to confirm a time to meet for the ME case.

"Doc, we had some obligations to attend to," said Randy. "It'll be after seven before we can head out there." The address was 20 miles out from South Hill. It would take them over an hour to return with the body. The scene, however, was only 15 to 20 minutes off of his route home.

"What if I meet you at the residence and examine the body there?" he asked.

"Sounds good to me."

Dr. Hardy aimed his white Jeep Cherokee toward Ebony Hill Road, heading south to the Lake Gaston area. The evening

September air in Virginia was warm. Fading sunlight highlighted the horizon with a pink glow. The scene was readily identified by the county police cruiser and a gray, Draper Funeral Home van in the driveway. Hardy walked to the front door carrying his makeshift ME bag, a plastic shopping bag with some disposable medical items. He had stocked it with supplies from the ER. The door opened as he approached.

"Dr. Hardy," greeted the detective inside the door. Detective Duffer stood a bit over six feet with a medium build. His age appeared similar to Dr. Hardy's. "This is the Banner family. The deceased is their daughter, Maureen."

Dr. Hardy greeted them briefly and the detective led him back to a hallway door.

"She's in here," he said as he opened the door. As they stepped inside, he continued. "She was out with friends last night. The family says they heard her come in about 1:30 AM. They just thought she was sleeping in until they checked on her this afternoon. She's been staying here with her parents since her divorce."

There was an adult female lying supine on the bed. Her eyes were open in a blank gaze upward and a sheet covered her lower body. She was clothed only in a cotton sleep shirt and her body was just above room temperature to touch. Her limbs were stiff but not completely rigid. Dr. Hardy placed a thermometer in her armpit. He noted that there was no gross evidence of physical injury. Whe he retrieved the thermometer, he studied the plastic probe cover. *I might can improvise a catheter with this* he thought. He punched a hole in the tip end with a needle.

Her pubic area was shaven along the perimeter with a tuff of short-trimmed hair centrally. The labia looked puffy, swollen with a purplish pink coloration. For the requested urine specimen, he inserted the probe cover into her urethral opening and advanced it to the hilt. Yellow liquid began trickling out into the specimen cup he held below.

"Bingo!" said Dr. Hardy. As he removed his "catheter", he noted some beige-colored mucous oozing from the vagina. A stained area on the bed sheet below her indicated that this drainage had been occurring before.

"When do you think she died, Doc?" asked Detective Duffer.

"My guess from rigor mortis and body temp, between six and eight AM."

"Okay. Oh, by the way, we found these on the night stand." He held out a plastic bag with lavender-colored tablets in it.

"What are they?"

"I suspect some home-made pharmaceuticals. Maybe meth."

"Oh. Well, we'll be testing her blood and urine for toxicologics. Synthetics may not show on the routine assays."

"I'm sending these to Richmond for identification."

"From the looks of it, she may have recently had some vigorous sexual activity."

"Well, I'll make note of that. Nothing I've found indicates that this is anything more that a recreational overdose. We'll see what the forensics show."

"Okay. I'll get my samples sent to the lab."

Dr. Hardy completed his journey home from work. His wife, Lucy, met him at the door. She was a smallish brunette originally from Florida. Their two daughters had both married in the past three years and they had become empty-nesters.

"You're sure late getting home," she said.

"Yeah. I had an ME case to work."

"Oh. Well, I got you a plate in the microwave when you're ready."

"Okay. Thanks."

"Anything interesting on the ME case?"

"It's probably just an overdose. I've got some samples to send to Richmond."

As he sat down to eat, he still queried himself over the significance of the engorged genitalia and the vaginal drainage. It didn't appear that she had been assaulted. Did some unbridled sexual activity contribute to her death?

Printed in the United States
by Baker & Taylor Publisher Services

Printed in the United States
by Baker & Taylor Publisher Services